Your Pastor…My Husband.

B.M. Hardin

ISBN-13: 978-0991528158

ISBN-10: 0991528158

Savvily Published LLC

Twitter: @Savvilypub

Facebook: www.facebook.com/savvilypub

Email: info@savvilypublished.com

This book is solely a work of fiction. All people, places and locals are strictly products of the author's imagination.

This story in no way or form describes the author's religions beliefs or personal evaluations.

3

..

~********~

Dedication

This book is dedicated to my beautiful readers.
I simply can not thank you all enough for supporting me
and my dream.

~**********~

6

Acknowledgments

First and foremost, I have to give thanks to God. Without him; I wouldn't be who I am today.

I'd also like to thank my family and friends. Your support and encouragement means the world to me. You challenge me and push me; and I am truly grateful for each and everyone of you.

I would also like to give a big thanks to Ms. Marie of "Edit Me Marie" for taking the time to look over and edit my work. I found you by mistake but I am truly thankful for all you have done.
www.editmemarie.com

To all of my readers and supporters...
Thank You again! Your support means the world to me and I hope that you can see it in my work!

B.M.Hardin

Your Pastor...My Husband

~***********~

Chapter One

I smiled as I admired my husband from the pulpit.

My husband, Pastor Shelton Cartwright, was still as charming, witty and handsome today as he had been the very first time I'd laid my eyes on him.

I still remembered it as though it had only happened yesterday.

A few years ago, I was going through some things.

To be honest, I was alive…but I wasn't actually living.

Some may not know what that means or feels like---but let me be the first to say that living a miserable life; was pretty much not worth living at all.

But after all was said and done, and when all else failed, there was only one place left for me to turn to…the church; God.

My very first time attending New Hope Missionary Church, Shelton took my breath away.

I remembered staring at him, hungrily, trying my best not to lust after his flesh during the church service.

But it was almost impossible.

I was having so many impure thoughts that I was afraid that at any moment God himself was going to personally get up from the throne, walk right out of Heaven, just to come and personally escort my lusting butt to the gates of Hell.

But Lord knows I was trying.

Who knew that a Pastor could be so darn sexy?

Shelton's stature made my mouth water.

His shoulders were broad and they were accompanied by his strong back and inviting muscular arms.

If I remembered correctly, I daydreamed about the way that his arms would feel wrapped tightly around me.

And he didn't have a wedding ring on his
finger...

Oh yes; all I needed was five minutes alone
with him!

His skin was the same exact color as warm,
sweet, mouth watering butterscotch.

Just looking at him caused me to lick my lips.

Shelton's tall frame moved comfortably,
effortlessly around the pulpit.

His facial hair was neatly groomed and since I
was only on the second pew; because all of the
other sinners had taken all of the empty seats
in the back, I was close enough to get a clear
view of his million dollar smile and his daring,
deep dimples.

Surely the Bible must have been referring to
him when it said that men were created after
God's own image.

This Pastor was f-i-n-e!

And I just had to have him.

The entire first part of the service, I struggled with trying to keep from wondering how he looked; with his clothes off.

Finally, I got myself together and thought about the Pastor on a different level.

I couldn't help but wonder why a handsome, middle aged man would take on such a big responsibility; such as being a Pastor of a church.

What made him want such an important role or title?

Why would he want to be the head of a church and such a huge task of being responsible for hundreds of people's salvation?

From looking at him, I assumed that he couldn't have been any older than thirty. Maybe thirty-five at the most.

When the lady sitting next to me finally initiated light conversation, I didn't hesitate to ask about the well dressed, stallion of a man standing behind the wooden podium.

From what I understood, he had just transferred to the church not even a month before, after the unexpected death of the late Pastor Armstrong.

She explained that at first there was quite the debate as to why he should take on the role; versus the job being given to one of the other older, more seasoned, Associate Pastors.

But nevertheless, he was voted in, with high hopes of bringing in the younger generation. And from the looks of it; he had done just that.

Looking around the church, it was a fairly good mixture of young and vibrant; as well as old and wise.

There were a tons of younger women in the crowd.

I was sure that most of the women were showing up just to see the main attraction…Pastor Shelton; and I as well; was taking a number and getting in line.

I was going to make it my business to come pay Pastor Shelton a little visit; as many Sunday's a month as I could.

But all jokes aside, and outside of his wicked good looks, once I got my mind out of the gutter and actually listened to the words that were coming out of his mouth; Pastor Shelton had this whole preaching thing on lock down! He was good...and I mean *real* good.

His words encouraged me; his words inspired me.

I'd heard good preaching before; but he got down on my level.

I understood him; I could relate to him.

His words soothe my troubled spirit and mended my broken heart and on that very day, I found myself standing in front of him at the altar---asking for salvation, and begging God for forgiveness.

All of that was five years ago.

Now, as you can see, I was still a work in progress.

I wasn't then nor am I currently the most *Christian* lady in the building.

I was nowhere near as saved as some or as holy as others, but I had come a mighty long way in just a few years time.

I wasn't brought up exactly in the church; I hadn't gone as much as I should have, so it all took some getting used to.

But Shelton had been more than patient with me.

He never judged me.

He'd always said that he knew my heart and he knew that I was trying my best.

And that was all that he could ever ask of me.

Even on that day, I had come broken and unholy.

Whether it was by fate, or by divine destiny...Pastor Shelton found favor in a little ole' wrench like me; and that was all I ever needed.

All I'd ever wanted was for someone to actually *see* me...and Shelton had.

In a way that no one ever had before.

Shelton had shown me a better way of living and for that I vowed to give him nothing less than my love, my loyalty and my respect for as long as there was breath in my body.

I'd always told him that he was my guardian angel; I was sure of it.

Shelton's sudden yell, brought my mind back from the *past*, and I focused on his *present* day sermon for only a second.

He was preaching about being out of the *will* of God and about having *free will*.

It was as if he was talking about the old me, which again caused my mind to wonder.

I tuned out my husband once again, and I started to reminisce about the past.

My Mama named me Maxine; but Maxi was what I preferred to be called.

Back then, couldn't nobody and I do mean nobody, tell me nothing that I didn't already know.

At least that's what I'd thought.

I had it all figured out; I had all of the answers.

A life of no worries was the way that I preferred to live and I did exactly what I wanted to do with no regrets.

It was my life...and I was going to live it the way that I wanted to.

Basically I was wild, stubborn and selfish; and I didn't care who knew it.

That's just the way that it was.

But the truth was that I was a young, naive girl, who thought that time was on her side; until I discovered some bad news...it wasn't.

Now, don't get me wrong; I wasn't all bad business.

I was down to earth, ambitious, and I was an all around Southern Bell; a drop dead gorgeous natural beauty.

My beauty was flawless, without a stitch of make-up; which couldn't boldly be said by too many folks these days.

I'm just saying.

I could cook like I was born in the 1920's and the way I could clean a house, would make you feel comfortable enough to eat right off of the floor...no five second rule necessary.

And on top of everything else, I was smart too. Graduated at the top of my class to be exact.

But somehow, none of that mattered when you used what was between your legs...ten times more than what was inside your head.

My whorish ways got me into more trouble than I bargained for.

I was always looking for the easy way out, even if I had to spread my legs to get it.

A long story short, I didn't mind being *used*; as long as I could use them in return.

But it didn't take long for me to learn that thinking that way; would never get me anywhere…except in a situation that I absolutely did not want to be in.

And I had my *ex-husband* to thank for teaching me that little lesson.

Yes, that's right; Shelton, the Pastor, was my

second husband; although that was my little

secret.

Neither he, nor anyone else for that matter,

knew anything about my past marriage.

I was taking that secret with me to my grave;

point...blank...period.

Sure, at times, I felt bad for keeping such a big

secret away from Shelton; but what he didn't

know---wouldn't hurt him.

Besides, for the most part, it really wasn't

worth mentioning.

You see, though it's sad to say this, but one of

the best days of my life was the day that the

police showed up on my doorstep to tell me

that my husband...the first one...was dead.

Someone had shot him down in the middle of

the street; leaving his lifeless body cold,

soaking in a puddle of his own blood.

To be honest, I wasn't surprised by his death.

I was more...what's the word... relieved.

Yeah, that's it.

Hell, if you really wanted to know the truth, I was just a little bit jealous that someone else had beaten me to the punch.

But thank God, more or less, that someone else had the nerve to kill him first.

Lord knows that I would have loved to have been the finger behind that trigger.

They never found his killer; at least I don't think.

But oh how I wanted to just tell them...

Thank You.

Yep...I'm dead serious too.

My ex-husbands' name *was* Richard Monroe; but in the streets he was known as Mr. Ricky.

Ricky was a part of everything; anything that was illegal.

From drugs and weapons; all the way down to trafficking women.

There wasn't much else to say except that Ricky loved playing dirty, and he always wanted a piece of the pie...money that is.

And you could bet on your life that he would do anything to get it.

And he would take it in any way that he could get it.

To him, money was everything.

To Ricky...money was power.

Actually; our entire marriage, *money* had been his *wife*...I was just his mistress.

Basically, Ricky was always about making a extra dollar.

I'll admit; at first, I was blinded by his wit, average good looks and not to mention all of the nice things that he could do and provide for me.

In the beginning, Ricky gave me all of his time and all of his money; and for me, that was enough.

Maybe it shouldn't have been---but it was.

But who could blame me?

Coming from a single parent home, with just my Mama, the attention of a man was something that I'd always lacked and secretly craved.

I never got the chance to know my Daddy.

Mama told me that he was killed while serving in the Army; only a month before I was born.

She'd said that he died a hero; defending his country and that was something that I should have been proud of.

Maybe so; but I'd always felt some kind of resentment toward him.

No, I didn't hate him or anything like that; after all, who could hate a hero?

But it would have been nice to have gotten to know him.

There were a ton of things that I would have appreciated learning from him...especially when it came to men.

There were just some things that Mama couldn't explain to me or teach me.

In my opinion, Mama never really got over losing Daddy and she never bothered to remarry.

Sure, she had a few *buddies* that she screwed in her spare time, but none of them had been important enough or even worth introducing to me…like…ever.

I mean, never had I witnessed Mama with a man.

For years, I grew up thinking that she was into women; until I was old enough for her to tell me that she had men to take care of her *needs*…when she wanted them to.

Still, none of them had ever made it to or inside of our home.

So, it was always just us.

That was it.

Now, let's be clear; Mama took damn good care of me.

I always had more than enough.

She was a strong, independent, and educated black woman and she tried her best to make sure that I would become the same.

Mama stayed on back, and despite my efforts, or lack thereof, she got me through high school and then pushed me through college.

Mama had done everything just right.

She had done everything that she could.

The only thing she couldn't do was give me the love that only my Daddy could have given me; that and the real scoop on what to expect when it came to men.

Mama said that Daddy had been her first...*everything*; and that he was the only man that she'd ever loved.

He was the only man that she had ever given the honor of claiming her or her heart, so understanding how men worked, was one of the only topics that Mama didn't have all of the answers to.

She had a few...but not many.

Mama always had so much to say, about everything...except when it came to her.

Only a year after I graduated from college, Mama died from breast cancer.

Apparently she'd known about it for years, but
had never bothered to mention it.

Not one single word to anybody; not even me,
her daughter, not even once.

And her sickness wasn't the only secret that it
appeared that Mama had kept from me.

Going through her diary, though she never
really came out and said it, it seemed as
though all along, my Daddy had been alive.

Her diary didn't say too much, but it had said
enough.

Her thoughts and comments ever so often
suggested that Daddy was indeed alive...and
not dead.

It was though she'd kept me away from him
for a reason.

Either that; or he had stayed away on purpose.

But he wasn't dead; I was sure of it.

Using a few learned skills from Mama, right
after her death, I'd even tried finding him by
name, and by every other piece of information
that Mama had ever given me about him.

But my attempts failed.

Either I was extremely unlucky or he really had died and I was just twisting Mama's privately written words, and making them something else.

But whether he was dead or not; I could only assume that Mama had her reasons for lying to me.

She always did everything for a reason and with purpose.

But I would have loved to have known the truth...about everything; especially hers.

Not that you could ever truly be prepared for death, but knowing the truth would have made things easier for me to deal with.

Or maybe it wouldn't have.

Nevertheless, with Mama gone, I was all alone.

I was all on my own and that was something that I had trouble getting used to.

The money that Mama left behind for me, eventually ran out.

Though I had a degree in Psychology, finding a job in my field wasn't as easy as I had hoped it would be.

So, I was stuck working dead end jobs that had absolutely nothing to do with my education or my training and I finally learned what it meant to struggle.

And let me tell you...the struggle was real!

No matter what I tried, no matter how hard I worked, I just couldn't seem to get ahead.

I was simply looking for a way out of my hard times...and that's where Ricky came in.

It was on my twenty-fifth birthday that I met Ricky at a local bar.

Ricky was splurging and the center of attention.

From the very beginning I was able to label the type of man that he was and make my assumptions.

It was obvious that he was into the street life; a drug dealer is what I initially assumed he was.

It was clear that he felt as though money made him a man; as though it gave him power.

His personality was bold…and loud.

He didn't have the slightest clue as to what *using your inside voice* actually meant; which was amongst the list of things that I hated about him.

He didn't have a single quality that I wanted in a future spouse; but he had exactly what I wanted for the time being…money.

All of my morals and all of the little things on my *list* went flying out the window whenever I saw a chance at stability; or whenever I thought that I had even the slightest chance at love…or at least something like it.

To this day, I still don't know why Ricky approached me that night, over all of the other horny, naked, tooth pick sized women that were throwing themselves at him.

But at the sight of me, he held up his finger to the bartender and headed in direction.

I was surprised.

I wasn't one of those slim and trim, water drinking, no meat---only lettuce eating, type of chicks.

Nor was I one of those women that made mouths fall open from being shaped like a *Coca-Cola* bottle...not at all.

I was more like two or three of those bottles...put together.

I had curves; the kind that you couldn't get rid of.

You know, the kind that could only be inherited; not the ones that could be sculpted...yep, those ones.

I had more than my share of breasts and booty and I had the triple D cup bra size and the double digit panties to prove it.

So, no, that night I hadn't been the slimmest woman in the crowd; but I was definitely the only woman in sight *acting* as though I had any kind of home training or any sense.

Although, in all actuality, and I'm just being honest; I was just like them.

My execution was just a little different.

I was a lady *first* and I had class; which meant that I wasn't overly thirsty for attention, well; at least I didn't show it.

I wasn't rubbing or grinding all over him; and I wasn't half naked either... all of my *rolls* were covered up.

Mama always reminded me that you could still be sexy…with your clothes on; that way, the man knows that he has to put in a little extra work to see what you were hiding underneath. Though I'd *remixed* her little saying to make it work for me; it still worked just as well.

They could see what was underneath alright; as long as the price was just right.

So, basically, I was a respectfully, and might I add, tastefully, dressed, classy hoe…well, more or less.

And I'm just keeping it real.

But the main thing was that I now had Ricky's interest...I could handle the rest.

Believe me, I was more than flattered that he chose the dark skinned big girl, over all of those typical light-skinned, long haired women.

So that night, of course, I gave him my undivided attention.

And to this day, that was one of the biggest mistakes that I'd ever made in my entire life.

For the next few months, Ricky wined and dined me, and before I knew it, a year had passed and we were standing at the Justice of Peace...getting married.

To be honest, I wouldn't say that I was ever madly in love with him; but I loved him enough.

And that was enough; at least I thought it was.

Of course, I was aware of his lifestyle but it had never caused us any problems and Ricky assured me that it never would.

He promised me that I would always come first...and like a dummy...I believed him.

But after we said *I do*, everything changed.

Ricky went from being sweet and charming; to downright hateful and disgusting.

He had gone from polite and respectful, to the most disrespectful man on the planet Earth.

Suddenly, Ricky was cruel, rude and obnoxious; all the time---and all at the same damn time!

He would embarrass me in front of his friends, cheat on me without so much as an apology and at times he would even attempt to put his hands on me…major mistake!

Mama didn't raise no fool…or no personal punching bag, and if nothing else I made sure that he'd known that much.

He would hit me…and I would hit his ass back! Apparently, Ricky wasn't as dumb as he looked.

He knew that physically, he would have himself a fight, so he was smart enough to pick and choose his battles.

But physical abuse was just one type of abuse.

The mental and emotional abuse that he continuously threw my way, was far worse than any punch or slap in the face on any given day.

Somehow, Ricky managed to make me feel like I was nothing every single time that I was in his presence.

So, here's the million dollar question...why didn't I leave him?

Hell, you tell me.

A part of me always hoped that things would get better, or at least go back to the way that they used to be.

The other part of me just didn't want to go back to being all alone.

For the life of me, I tried to salvage my marriage and uphold my vows, but no matter how hard I tried, things never changed.

For almost two years, they stayed the same.

And then one day, just as I was starting to get enough courage and nerve to walk away; something *amazing* happened...

Ricky was dead.

I would be lying if I said that I didn't feel a thing and that I wasn't at all sad or hurt...

I was...in a way.

But as Ricky and his charcoal black casket made their way into the ground, my heart skipped a beat, from excitement and in the inside, I secretly smiled...

I was free!

Ain't God good?

Ding, dong that wicked dirt bag was dead!

Yeah...it's as bad as it sounds.

But I was so happy that he was gone.

Hell, I wanted to throw myself a *Happy Widow* party, but I decided that it would have been just a little bit rude.

So, I simply celebrated in silence and in secret.

Ricky was a horrible husband when he was alive, but he made one hell of a decent one once he was gone.

He didn't have a 401 k plan or an insurance policy or anything like that; but he did have three cars, not including mine, a house that was paid for and a safe with over $200,000 in it. So, after burying him the cheapest way possible, I sold everything except my car.

I didn't want anything to remind me of him or the torture that he'd put me through.

Almost two months after his death and after it was all said and done, I took the money and got as far away from my past as I possibly could.

That's how I ended up here.

I left the only place I'd ever known; Arlington, Texas, and settled thousands of miles away, way down in the *country* parts of South Carolina.

I didn't know a soul and with almost half a million dollars, I bought a small, cozy house for little of nothing and focused on making a better life for myself.

All I wanted was a fresh start.

All I needed was a clean slate.

I was only twenty-eight years old then, and I had plenty of time to turn my life around and become the woman that Mama always wanted me to be.

No one knew me, no one would judge me.

I vowed to pretend as though my past never existed; as though none of it ever happened.

So, to this day, I'd never mentioned any of it, to anyone---ever.

Though then, I didn't exactly need the money, Mama always said that *an idle mind was the Devil's playground,* so I got lucky and I found a small counseling job.

Funny isn't it; I was giving advice and encouragement to someone else, when I desperately needed it for myself.

I was so heart broken, lost and confused.

I needed someone to be there for me; but I didn't have anyone to talk to.

There was no one to tell me that things were going to be okay or to give me hope for the future.

And then it hit me.

One morning I got up, got dressed and my car led the way to a big white church only about a mile away from my house…and that's the day that my life was changed forever.

That's how I ended up at the church.

And that's how I ended up *here*.

Now, I was married to a Pastor; a wonderful man of God, who treated me like I was nothing less than pure gold.

I had a beautiful daughter, and I was surrounded by some of the most loving people that God had ever created.

I was now on the right path.

I mean, aside from a few secrets from my past, a little cursing here and there, and tad bit of wine sipping every blue moon, I was darn near a saint.

I made one pretty good Pastor's wife, if I must say so myself.

For the first time ever; life was good.

"You preached one heck of a sermon today Pastor Cartwright," I smiled at my husband as he leaned over to peck my lips.

Church was finally over and Shelton's first stop was me, on the front pew; just like always.

"Well, thank you Mrs. Cartwright," Shelton responded sarcastically, or maybe he was being just a little bit cocky.

Blame it on my degree in Psychology, but I was almost certain that there was another side to my husband that I had yet to see or one that I would never get to know.

It was just something about him.

Something about Shelton was just so dark and mysterious, that I often wondered about his life before he started preaching the Gospel.

It was just the way he said certain things, or maybe it was the way that he reacted to certain situations…before his man of faith would step in the way.

I was sure that he had a temper problem; though he made it his business to never let me see it.

I was sure that he had anger issues; but he was very good at hiding them.

And though it may not mean a whole lot to mention this, but I was at least 80 percent sure that at some point in time or at some period in his life...Shelton had been a porn star---or hell, a male stripper or something.

The way he made love to me just didn't seem normal; not for a Pastor that is.

It was rough; it was dirty.

It had street, hood, thug---something, written all over *it*.

I couldn't quite put *it* into words, but *it* surely didn't say a man of the cloth.

Granted that even Pastor's have a past, and that most of them are sinners for quite some time, before they turned into saints, but my husband, Shelton, acted as though he was born with a Bible in his hands.

He never, ever wanted to talk about his past. It was almost as if he'd tried to erase it or delete it; just as I had done with my own. Oh, and don't let me start asking questions; Shelton would get a real bad case of amnesia…real quick.

Let him tell it, he was the same man that he had always been; but I wasn't buying it.

Still yet, no matter how many questions I asked him; he refused to go into detail about anything in his past other than stories about being a orphan and foster child.

"What do you want for dinner?" I asked Shelton, as we continued to greet other members of the church.

The church had every bit of five hundred active members, if not more, and they absolutely adored him.

The members were trustworthy and dependable and they were the closest thing that either of us had to family.

There was nothing that they wouldn't do for their Pastor, and Shelton spent every day showing them his appreciation.

He was so dedicated to the members and to the church more than I could even explain.

On most days, I was more like his side chick; and the church was his main *thang*.

I swear the church and I always seemed to be battling for that number one spot in Shelton's life.

Needless to say, most of the time...I lost.

But I'd rather have a God fearing man, spending his time in church, any day, versus a man that spent most of his time in the streets.

Some days, though it had been years, it was still hard to believe that I was a Pastor's wife.

Mama would have been so proud of me.

Never had I imagined that this is where I would end up; but this is where I was.

And this was where I would always be.

Shelton shrugged his shoulders as the answer to my question and then followed his gesture with a small smirk.

He was always so difficult, but I wouldn't trade him or my life with him, for anything else in this world.

And that---was a fact.

After arriving at our home, only a block away from the church, Shelton undressed and he and our daughter, scampered outside for some sunlight and fresh air.

I laughed aloud as I watched them from the kitchen window.

Our baby girl, Mackenzie, had just learned to walk, and she wobbled toward Shelton.

It took awhile, but she finally reached him, just before falling into Shelton's open arms.

Shelton's face lit up as bright as one of the stars that had led the slaves to freedom.

He kissed her as both of them collapsed onto the ground.

It was barely Spring, but the sun was definitely making its presence known.

Glancing out at them one last time, I headed to the refrigerator to figure out what we were going to have for Sunday dinner.

Here, unlike in Texas, Sunday dinner was a big thing; it was everything.

It was the one day of week that these country women decided to pull out all of their cooking secrets and make their finest dishes.

Though I was always top notch in the kitchen, the Mothers of the church had done their share of teaching me some of their famous recipes.

I'd put my own twists to them; and now they were just a little bit better.

Just as I'd placed the chicken breasts in warm water, the house phone began to ring.

"Hello?"

"Hello, is Pastor Shelton available?" the voice asked on the other end of the phone.

The voice didn't sound familiar, so I asked for a name.

The caller stuttered and then called himself John; but he and I both knew that *John* wasn't his real name.

"Shelton...telephone!" I screamed from the kitchen window.

I heard the caller curse saying the word *damn*.

I guess maybe I could have muted the phone before I screamed.

But one thing was for sure; just from his comment; this *John* fellow, most likely wasn't a Pastor.

Shelton hurried inside and handed Mackenzie off to me.

"Hello," Shelton responded after he kissed my cheek.

I settled our daughter into her feeding chair, though my focus was still on my husband.

I noticed that he was still standing in the same spot, somewhat frozen and in silence.

All of a sudden, he appeared to be rather tensed.

Shelton breathed heavily but said nothing.

Now that was a first.

Shelton was always talking; and I do mean always...even in his sleep.

I had never heard him, or seen him so quiet, and from the look on his face, though he desperately tried to hide it; I could tell that something was wrong.

Shelton noticed that I was staring at him; which seemed to make him even more uncomfortable.

And with that, Shelton excused himself from the kitchen, with no words, only a look and a slight nod.

Hmm...who was that?

~**********~

~Life will always be exactly what it's meant to be. Never be afraid to try something new. Never be afraid to try again~
Anonymous

Chapter Two

"Maxine? Maxi, are you awake?" Shelton whispered.

Am I awake; really, did he just ask me that question?

After all, who could sleep with a ten inch *pole* piercing them in the lower part of their back? Not saying a word, I continued to lie still, though I knew that he was going to *take* what he wanted anyway.

I didn't mind being intimate with my husband. Actually, in the words of the old folks...it was the best thing since *cooked crack*.

But, seriously, I always had to prepare myself mentally, and physically; before I went *there* with Shelton.

Before him, I used to think that I was every man's *wet dream* in the bedroom; at least that was how most of them would react to my sex or make me feel after I *blessed* them with my *goodies*.

But not Shelton.

He was a *monster* between the sheets, and for any trick that I thought I had; he had something better.

As I said, his sexual side just didn't quite match him as a person and definitely not as a Pastor.

The sweet, humble and caring man that he was on a day to day basis was nowhere in sight when it came to *getting down*…with the *get down*.

Behind closed doors, the bedroom door particularly; Shelton was a completely different man.

He was aggressive, controlling and even a little bit scary at times.

He was always so gentle and humble, but in the bedroom, Shelton wanted to bend me, flip me, tackle me, smack me; hell anything he felt like doing in the heat of the moment.

There were so many times that I wanted to stop him right in the middle of it all and ask him:

Fool, have forgotten that I'm team big girl?

I mean, I'm just saying!

But Shelton could have probably cared less.

As he tugged on my panties, I internally gave myself a little pep talk for the *sexual beating* that me...and my *Gangsta'* were about to endure.

After a few more seconds of panty fondling, Shelton ripped them clean off at the sides, almost causing me to jump in fright.

Uh oh, here we go.

With my back still toward him, I still remained silent; not because I thought he would give up...I knew that he wouldn't.

But at least by staying quiet, it would give me just a few more minutes of foreplay and a chance to get my mind right.

As his hands roamed freely, hungrily all over my body, his fingers eventually found their way to my clitoris and he began to nibble on my ear.

Darn it...now, he know that that's my spot!

"Maxi," he whispered again between light kisses and sucks.

Though I tried to fight it, I was becoming more and more aroused by the seconds and my most *prized possession* began to effortlessly and *disobediently*, release *her* sweet juices, soaking Shelton's fingers with pure evidence of my arousal.

Unable to keep my quiet streak, a small moan escaped from my lips without my permission.

Aw, hell...it's on now!

That small moan was exactly what Shelton was waiting to hear.

He forcefully rolled me onto my back and without hesitation; he damn near swallowed my lips whole.

Shelton kissed me with so much passion; so much force.

I'm telling you; it was the complete opposite of those little, gentle, church kisses that he laid on me during the day time.

His kisses behind closed doors were hungry, savage-like; and he just wouldn't stop until *victory* was won...well until...you know.

My participation was at a minimum; knowing that he didn't need, and probably didn't even want my *help*.

"I love you," my husband managed to sneak in between his constant pecks of affection.

I didn't respond because I knew that all of his display of affection was time sensitive; and that all of his sweetness was about to expire in only a matter of seconds.

I was right.

"Who's is *it*?" Shelton asked as he *entered* me.

Told you...

Mr. Nice Guy was gone.

I positioned myself just right, to prepare myself for the *ride*.

"I asked you a question, and I'm not going to
ask you again bi---, um, who's it huh...who's is
it!" Shelton demanded an answer as he began
to stroke, slowly.

Lord, I almost laughed.

It just tickled me that no matter how
aggressive and crazy he became during sex; he
never cursed...or used the word *pussy*.

As you can see, I still did just a *little* cursing;
not around Shelton of course.

But never, ever, had I heard Shelton use foul
language.

Guess that was expected from a man of his
importance or caliber.

"It's yours *daddy*," I stroked his ego as he
continued to stroke my *kitty*; well...more like
my *cougar*.

He smiled, yet his hands found their way to
my throat and he began to squeeze.

Shelton choked me as he continued to *swim* in
my *pool of ecstasy*.

A time or two I had to tap his hands to let him know that I couldn't breathe.

But my taps were ignored.

Still, it wasn't until on his own time, that Shelton finally released my throat.

I gasped for air, but Shelton didn't show a bit of concern for me; or my breathing.

Mumbling to himself as he placed my legs on his shoulders, slid both of his hands securely under all of my booty, and held onto it firmly.

All the while, his *manhood* remained inside of me.

I moaned with every move that he made.

Some by choice; others out of nothing but pure pleasure.

Although, I couldn't quite keep up with him, I still very much enjoyed the way that he made me feel.

"Who's been touching you?" Shelton asked as my moaning came to a halt.

He knew that no one had even come close to touching me; yet he always asked this question during sex.

It was as if it made him *sexually angry*; if there was such a thing.

It was as though it was his duty to punish me or teach me some type of lesson.

"Nobody," I said in a low, teasingly voice.

"Um, huh, I don't believe you. So, I'll ask you again. Who's been touching you Maxine? And this time, you'd better not lie to me! You belong to me, and don't you ever forget that, you hear me?" he asked me, just shy of a yell.

His *pounds of punishment* had grown more intense and his grip underneath me had suddenly tightened.

I closed my eyes as I focused on his thick, dipped in honey, *rod of desire*, as it rammed in and out of me, torturing my insides and the bottom of my stomach.

I could no longer be *cute* about the situation. My mouth opened wide and I began to yell,

and call him everything but a child of God---
which only turned him on even more.

As the temperature of my body began to rise,
our bodies instinctively began to rock to the
same unheard tune, and the room appeared to
be closing in on us.

Shelton continued to torment me with his
words and with his *copper-colored magic stick,* as
I turned the corner onto *Orgasm Avenue.*

Somehow, abruptly, and with one quick
motion our naked bodies went from bouncing
up and down on our bed, to rolling around on
the cold hardwood floor.

It wasn't long after that, that I found myself on
my knees, with Shelton pounding away behind
me.

His grunts filled the empty spaces of the room,
as his pumps became faster and faster.

Frantically, I grabbed a hold of the overpriced
rug that was placed underneath our bed.

I was almost at the finish line so I closed my
eyes and concentrated on the feeling of

Shelton's warm *wood*, as if *destroyed* everything in its path as it terrorized my insides.

He tried to hold on, but he couldn't.

Shelton started to howl and then soon after, he filled my insides with his sweet, soothing cum, and I was right behind him.

My mouth released a high pitched scream as my body released about a gallon of my *juices of satisfaction.*

We both collapsed onto the floor, exhausted and trying to catch our breaths.

Once we'd cooled down, Shelton pulled me close to him and wrapped me tightly in his arms.

As we snuggled, and Shelton began to snore, I found myself thinking about him.

I'd had a lot of sex in my day, but none had ever compared to Shelton's.

That was a good thing.

Whether couples wanted to admit it or not, sex was at least 50%, if not more, of a *healthy* relationship.

Well that applied to most people and to most relationships.

Hell, sex had been a part of every single one of my relationships...and none of them were anywhere near healthy.

Except with Shelton of course.

During my college years, it was as though I was passing around my panties, more than I was passing my exams.

With so many men in one place, I was determined to make someone fall in love with me; even if that meant that I had to give out a few *samples*.

Out of many, eventually, there was one who actually fell in love with me.

The only problem was that I didn't love him back.

To be honest, of the few guys that I was dealing with at the time...he was actually the one I liked the least.

And when the truth came out, I ended up paying a terrible price for it.

I was a junior in college at the time and everyone wanted a piece of the star basketball, senior player---Trent Hall.

Just like all of the other girls, I wanted him for his popularity; and I assumed that he wanted me for what was up under my skirt.

He did...but he also wanted more.

Trent was different.

He was what I should have been looking for in a man, but at the time, my priorities were more than messed up.

After a few weeks of *fooling* around, he wanted to make things a little more official.

I agreed but not because I wanted to; but because I wasn't doing anything else at the time.

And because he was actually nice to me and I didn't want to hurt his feelings.

Yet, no matter how hard I tried, I just couldn't get into him on that level nor could I be faithful to him.

I tried to keep all my of *goodies* in my *pussy purse,* but time after time---I failed.

One night, Trent caught me entertaining the attention, kisses, and touches of one of his team mates.

We hadn't actually had sex yet; but we were definitely on our way.

For a few days, he refused to talk to me, to hear my side of the story or at least allow me to tell him a few lies and apologize.

Just as I was about to stop trying to be nice, finally, he invited me over to his college apartment to talk.

Something told me not to go, to just let it be... but I didn't listen.

Lord knows I wish I had.

To make a long story short, Trent and a few of his friends, including the one that I was going to have sex with a few nights before, raped me. And I mean they took turns with me over and over again; until neither one of them could no longer get an erection.

And that wasn't even the worst part.

The worst part of it all was...

No one believed me.

They all stuck to the same story; the same lie.

They'd said that I wanted to do it.

Everyone that the police spoke to agreed that I was a little on the promiscuous side; and just like that, they had gotten away with a crime.

The case was closed.

You'd think that after all of that, I would have slowed down; but actually I got worse.

I started sleeping with professors, breaking up happy homes and all of that other nonsense.

I figured what was the point in caring about others...no one cared about me.

Well, except Mama...but sometimes *just* her love just wasn't enough.

Shaking away my thoughts, a sudden chill came over my body.

I moved Shelton's arms, only for a second to grab pillows and a blanket from the bed.

After I made myself comfortable on the floor, I turned to face my sleeping husband.

If only he knew the truth about the woman that he was married to.

I wondered if things would be the same.

Even though I wasn't that woman anymore, its always good to know the reviews or the history on something; before you *purchased* it.

I'd lied and told Shelton that he was only the second man that I'd ever had sex with.

I mean, in a way, he was…after you added another hundred to it.

And I was lucky if that was even accurate.

There were so many things in my past that I wasn't proud of; which was why there were just some things about me that Shelton would never know.

And I could only assume that Shelton felt the same way about his past.

From the way that he acted when I tried to get to know the *old* him, I knew that he'd probably done a few things, like me, that he wished that he could take back.

Though I'd always wondered about who he used to be, at that moment, I decided that wanting to know the old him was useless.

Who he was now was more than enough for me.

And who I had become, was obviously enough for him.

What I didn't know; wouldn't hurt me...

At least that was what I'd thought...

~***~

"Shelton, I forgot to ask you, who was that on the phone the other day; that *John* man?" I asked Shelton the next morning, after we had taken a shower together.

It had crossed my mind all of a sudden.

Shelton was hesitant---which was something that he never was.

"Oh, honey that was nobody that you need to be concerned about. Someone I knew way back in the day, when I was in my early twenties.

He'd gotten wind that I was a Pastor now, and reached out to me. That was all," Shelton answered with his back toward me.

Liar.

"Oh, he was from your past? Was he a friend? I would love to meet him. Is he married? Maybe we could do Sunday dinner," I proclaimed.

"No," he responded.

"No…what?"

"No he wasn't…isn't a friend; he's just someone I knew back then. Let it go Maxi," Shelton concluded the conversation with a fake smile, dressed, kissed me and then exited the room.

See, I was trying to be nice and not be so nosy; but to hell with that!

Scratch what I said last night…this Pastor had something to hide…and I was going to find out just what it was.

What could it possibly about his past that he didn't want me to know about?

It couldn't be any worse than mine...or could it?

I mean, of course I really didn't have any grounds to pry; especially since I had more secrets than a little bit in my back pocket, but at least I wasn't walking around pretending to be perfect.

Shelton, on the other hand, acted as though there was nothing about his past that he was ashamed of.

Let him tell it; he found God, found the church and then found me...the end.

Just who did he think that he was fooling?

Don't get me wrong, Shelton was a good man and I couldn't ask for a better husband and father for Mackenzie.

I mean, he loved me unconditionally.

He made me feel like I was the smartest, prettiest, sexiest woman in the world.

He complimented me regularly.

Shelton made sure that I always had everything that I needed; whether it was physically, financially, emotionally...and of course, sexually.

But Shelton was like; this big puzzle.

The one that takes you weeks to put together and then right at the end, you find out that you are missing a few of the pieces.

That's how I felt about Shelton; and I was just dying to find those missing pieces.

I watched him get into his white Lincoln town car; the one that the church members had just gotten him as a Pastor's Anniversary gift.

He drove away in a hurry.

I could only assume that he was heading to the church; either that or he was meeting someone from the church...or about church.

Long story short; I didn't expect to see him again until later on that evening.

It was only about eight o'clock in the morning but I was more than certain that he wouldn't be arriving back home until around seven or eight o'clock that night.

I headed to check on our daughter who was sleeping a little later than usual.

Quietly, I admired her for a moment.

She looked so much like Shelton; a girl version of course.

My darling baby girl didn't look a thing like me.

I was dark skinned but she was a cinnamon-honey shade of brown, almost like Shelton.

Her hair was soft and curly, just like his, and she even managed to get his bold, condemning brown eyes.

She looked like him when she smiled and when she cried.

She even looked like him as she slept.

And she absolutely loved him too.

She was the true definition of a daddy's girl; but I didn't mind.

To be honest, I somewhat envied the fact that she actually had a choice in the matter.

But though I wasn't exactly her first choice, she still loved me and she knew that her mama loved her.

There was nothing in the world that I wouldn't do for her and I made sure that she knew that.

I wanted our bond to be just like the one that Mama and I once shared---minus the lies.

Mama and I were so close that no one and I do mean no one, believed that we were mother and daughter.

We acted not only like sisters, but also like best friends.

We could talk about anything, everything and whenever I needed her she was always right there.

I guess in a sense she had to be.

We were all that each other had.

Her mother, my grandmother, whom I'd also never met, had disowned her for running off and getting married to my Daddy at such a young age.

Mama never saw or heard from her parents or any of her siblings again...though I think that it had been strictly Mama's choice.

I wasn't sure, but I thought I remembered Mama saying that they were somewhere in Mississippi, but she would never say much else about them.

She never even called them by name.

Mama married my Daddy and ran off to Korea, then to Germany, and from there they ended up in Texas, at least that was the story that Mama had always told me.

When Daddy was called to be stationed overseas, again, Mama found out that she was pregnant with me and they both decided that it was best if she stayed behind.

Unfortunately, Daddy never returned to us, and as I learned, it wasn't by death; maybe it was by choice.

Whether the choice was his or hers, either way, from then on it was just Mama and I; living and battling life one day at a time.

Just the two of us.

Truth be told, I admired Mama's strength.

Never had I seen her begging for handouts.

She did what she had to do to make sure that I...we were okay.

Even when times got hard, she never gave up. Tucking in her *tail* and running back home to Mississippi just wasn't an option for her, and she made sure that she would never have to. I watched Mama work her *tail* off and she became one hell of a lawyer when I was about ten, and from there, there was no turning back. We lived a good life, and everything turned out to be just fine.

It was just us.

No family, a few friends, but mostly, we only had each other; until God took Mama away from me.

I had always heard that when people died too young or before their time that it wasn't because you had done something wrong.

It wasn't because you were being punished or because God wanted to hurt you.

God only took them to Heaven…because he needed them more.

And that just had to be true about Mama.

I could only imagine Mama in Heaven, singing, and probably even directing the choir of angels. She had the most beautiful, heaven sent voice I'd ever heard.

I couldn't blame God for wanting to hear her sing every single day.

That was truly something I missed the most about her.

Coming back to reality, I glanced down at my sleeping little angel again.

It saddened me that she would never get to meet any of her grandparents.

My parents were both dead; well, maybe one was still alive, but hell if he was, I didn't know where he was or enough information about him to find him.

Shelton didn't know who his parents were at all.

From what he'd told me, his mother had given him up at birth; he had never even seen a picture of her, nor did he know her name.

He was adopted by a couple as a baby and a few years later, when the couple divorced, he ended up right back in the system.

He had thought for years that they were his real parents and that they just hadn't wanted him anymore, only to find out in his teens that they hadn't been his parents at all.

He was told that a young woman came into a hospital, used a fake name, gave birth to a baby boy and as soon as the doctors were out of sight, she left him there, never to return for him.

I actually felt sorry for Shelton.

I couldn't imagine how he must have felt as a child.

Not having a father is one thing---but not having a mother was another.

There was nothing; no one like your Mama.

But despite it all; he had turned out alright.

Shelton wasn't angry about it either; he'd

actually said that whoever his parents were,

that he only hoped that they were well and

that he had forgiven them a long time ago.

He said had it not been for what they had

done; he may not have become the man that he

was today.

Maybe he was right.

I guessed that was why he loved our daughter

with every fiber in his body and that was yet

another thing that was so damn sexy about

him.

Nothing was sexier about a man, than the love

that he had for his kids or his mother.

It had always been a major turn on in my book.

As Mackenzie cooed, I decided to let her sleep

a little while longer.

At least with her asleep, I could have some

time to myself; some time where I wasn't being

someone's mommy...or someone's wife.

I headed to the kitchen to my secret stash.

I poured myself a glass of wine and headed outside to the front porch.

It was definitely too early for a drink, but after last night, I surely needed one.

Drinking was another one of my little secrets that Shelton didn't know about.

He would probably die if he knew that I took a sip of wine every now and then, after all, I was a Pastor's wife.

I was working on letting it go; slowly but surely.

It wasn't nearly as bad as it used to be; or as bad as it was when I was with Ricky.

I sat down on the first step, as the early morning sun caressed my face and softly *kissed* my cheeks.

It wasn't until I was settled that I noticed the vase full of roses, with a note sticking out of them.

Shelton.

When had he had time to do this?

I sat down my glass and picked up the vase instead.

Smiling, I read the note card.

"Every day, I fall more and more in love with you. When God created you, he must have had me on his mind. You are everything I have ever wanted. My life would be nothing without you. I love you, Shelton."

This man always knew just what to do and say to put a smile on my face.

He was the *perfect* husband.

Loving, caring, and he did pretty much everything just right.

Pastor Shelton was affectionate, a great listener and everything he did was from the heart.

He was so thoughtful and didn't mind putting his heart on the line for anyone, any day, at any time.

Briefly, I thought about the day that he proposed to me.

We'd only being seeing each other for about six months before he popped the big question.

After my first initial visit, I vowed that church, that church particularly, was where I would be every Sunday.

It wasn't until my fourth Sunday attending that Shelton finally asked me out on our first date.

At first, I declined.

Not because I wanted to; Lord knows that I wanted to do more than go on a simple date with him, though I knew taking him home for a *nightcap*, would be out of the question.

But I declined because the truth was...I just wasn't ready.

I had more *baggage* than I wanted or need; but Shelton was persistent.

He just wouldn't take *no* for an answer.

He assured me that he wanted nothing from me, and of course, I was sure that he was a man of his word.

Our first date was like Heaven on Earth.

I found it refreshing that he had a sense of humor, one unlike I'd ever seen.

I laughed at all of his jokes, on purpose, and
not only because I was trying to be nice.
He was nothing like I imagined a Pastor to be;
nothing at all.
I assumed that the whole dinner would be
about Jesus, church and sinners…but it was the
complete opposite.
Shelton had real conversation, interesting
topics, and not once did he mention religion.
He wowed me the entire night, leaving me
breathless and in complete awe of him.
And even though he didn't quite know it yet---
he already had me under his spell.
That night was the first of many nights and
dates to come.
We continued to date and spent every day
around each other; whether it was at the
church or in private.
I'll admit; it felt damn good to be around a
man who didn't want anything in return.
He didn't require my panties; he only required
my presence.

He didn't want to lay with me, he'd much
rather pray for me or pray with me.
For the first time, I could truly say that I was in
love.
And then came that glorious day.
It was a cold, windy, December night;
December the 14th to be exact.
The church was supposed to be in revival and I
promised Shelton that I would come by right
after work.
So many times I thought about bypassing the
church and going straight home, but thank
God I didn't.
Tired, and pressing on anyway, I entered the
church only to find that the church wasn't
having a revival at all.
Actually; the sanctuary was empty.
Checking my watch, I was sure that the service
should have still been carrying on but the
proof was in the pudding.
The church was deserted.

Yet, there was a parking lot full of cars outside,
so I headed to the fellowship hall.
After all, the Mothers of the church were
known to whip up a quick meal at the drop of
a dime.
My mouth started to water just thinking about
it.
I could hear the chatter from down the hall,
and as I walked through the doors, my face lit
up like a small child's on Christmas morning.
Immediately, I spotted Shelton.
He was wearing an all-white three piece suit,
with a tangerine bow tie.
The room was decorated with tons of tangerine
and white balloons and flowers.
My favorite colors.
Frozen, I couldn't do a thing but smile as the
entire room became noiseless and Shelton
inched in my direction.
He was smiling from ear to ear as he neared
me, and as he reached for my hands.
The look on his face was priceless.

It was a look that I had never seen before.

It was a look of love, respect, honor…hell it even had just a pinch of excitement, as if he had won the lottery, jackpot or something. "Maxi---Maxine, you are like a breath of fresh air. Never have I met a woman that makes me feel so complete; that makes me feel like I'm the luckiest man in the world. You support me, you encourage me, and I would be crazy not to make you my wife. So, Maxine Renee Lowery…will you do me the honor and make me the happiest man in the world by becoming my wife?" Shelton asked now on his knees, holding a red velvet box in one hand and a two carat diamond ring in the other.

The flood gates of Heaven opened and tears began to flow rapidly down my face.

Who would have thought?

He loved me…I was nothing, broken, still yet he loved me?

My head nodded *yes* before I could even open my mouth.

The room ranged with applause and Shelton swiftly placed the ring on my finger and stood to his feet.

That night, for the first time...he kissed me.

Call me silly, but I'm almost positive that I heard Mama singing all the way from Heaven, as the fireworks of my heart exploded with nothing but pure happiness.

That was indeed on the list of best nights of my life.

And only three months later came the best day of my life, my wedding day; the day I became Mrs. Shelton Jacobs Cartwright.

Mackenzie's crying startled me and the thoughts of my wedding rushed out of my head as I rushed inside to the aid of my wailing daughter.

My life was perfect.

I had a beautiful daughter, a husband that loved me, and a church full of people who loved me just like family.

Who could ask for anything more?

With my baby in my arms, I rushed to answer the ringing phone.

"Hello?" I asked, placing my daughter on the floor, watching her scurry away like a little cockroach.

Dead Silence.

"Hello, can I help you?" I asked again, but the only response I received was the dial tone. Shrugging my shoulders, I decided that I was in need of a little *retail therapy*.

Sitting around the house had done nothing for my already plus sized figure, so it was about time that I got out and about, even if it was just for a little while.

So, after feeding Mackenzie, and once we were dressed, I loaded our necessary belongings, and my vase of roses, into the car and we headed to the highway for a three hour drive to Charlotte, North Carolina.

I'd only been to North Carolina twice; with Shelton, on church business.

But we were able to visit a few places, including their malls and let's just say; I was a fan.

Besides, a long ride and fresh air was just what I needed.

With music and the comfort of my hair blowing in the wind, I turned a three hour trip into barely two.

Entering the mall, I thought to call Shelton, but I figured that he was probably too busy, and there was really no need to bother him.

Besides, I was sure that he wouldn't answer, so placing the phone in my purse; it was time to do some serious *shopping damage*.

Mother and daughter time with my daughter was just what the doctor ordered.

We shopped a little, had lunch and then shopped some more.

Before I knew it, time had gotten away from me and it was now almost six o'clock in the evening, and past time for us to head back home.

Hopefully, I would still beat Shelton home and at least attempt to get dinner started.

After loading Mackenzie into the car, I headed to the trunk to load it with the stroller and over two thousand dollars' worth of stuff that technically we didn't even need.

I heard the footsteps but I didn't think anything of it.

I was minding my own business, when all of a sudden…

Everything went pitch black.

~***~

I woke up with an excruciating headache.

Immediately, I noticed that I was in a hospital and attempted to lift up but the heaviness of my head weighed me back down.

"Shelton?" I called.

"Yes baby, I'm here," he answered almost too soon.

He approached me in a panic.

"Baby, why am I in a hospital? What happened? Where is Kenzie?" I questioned him.

"Relax baby," Shelton said softly, and I noticed the woman doctor, standing in the corner.

"Hello Mrs. Cartwright, how are you feeling?" she questioned me but I didn't respond.

"You took quite a few blows to the head; it's a miracle that you are still alive," the tiny Chinese doctor proclaimed.

What the hell was she talking about it?

Blows to the head?

Who's head?

Huh?

"Where is my daughter?" I asked again.

"She's fine," Shelton answered bluntly.

"Well, we want to keep you for a few more days. Just to keep an eye on you. No serious damage, well no permanent damage was done. Someone was definitely praying for you," the doctor said with a smile and nodded in Shelton's direction.

I looked at Shelton as he watched the doctor exit the room and then he turned to face me. "What in the hell were you thinking Maxine? You don't come all the way to another state without telling me!" Shelton screamed, startling me.

Did he just curse?

I had never heard him curse before.

I mean, technically, *Hell* wasn't a curse word; but as Mama used to say...it all depends on how you used it.

This must be serious.

"This was the dumbest thing you have ever done! I could have lost you today! How could you have been so stupid?" Shelton continued his rant of anger.

I felt my lips begin to tremble and soon after, I started to cry.

He was upset...okay I get that, and maybe he was even a little frightened but still, why was he speaking to me this way?

From the looks of it...I was the damn victim!

I didn't even know what was going on, so why
was he blaming me?

"What happened?" I sobbed, and reached for
my husband's hand, relieved that he didn't
snatch it away.

Why did I feel like I had done something wrong?
All I wanted to do was get away and enjoy my day.
But no, I end up laying in a damn hospital bed!

"You were attacked. They hit you numerous of
times in the back of the head. The doctors
couldn't quite make out what the attacker
struck you with, but they are assuming that it
was maybe something as simple as a stick or a
piece of wood. When you were found, you
were unconscious and laying with blood all
over you. Mackenzie was untouched, in her car
seat, screaming at the top of her lungs. They
thought that maybe it was a mugging, yet they
didn't take anything. They didn't touch a
single one of your purchases nor did they take
any of your credit cards and over three
hundred dollars of cash was still in your wallet

when the police arrived on the scene. So, they are unsure of a motive, or as to why you were the target of such a vicious attack---except if it was a personal. The police said the only explanation seemed to be if the attacker knew you on a personal level and attacked you for their own personal reasons. Imagine how I felt when I received a random phone call from the police stating that my wife and daughter were being rushed to the hospital, three hours away, and that they were unsure if my wife was going to make it. I'm supposed to be able to protect you and Kenzie. How can I protect you if I don't know where you are? If I'd lost you, either of you, I don't know what I would have done," Shelton exhaled and sat down in the chair beside the bed.

Huh?

I was so confused.

Why would anyone attack me, a mother with her child, minding her own business?

And personal...how could the attack be personal?

No one even knew where I was going.

"There's nothing wrong right, or no one that would want to hurt you or nothing that I should know about---anything?" Shelton questioned me.

"Huh, no, what does that mean? I don't know a soul other than you and the church members in South Carolina and I damn...excuse me, darn sure don't know anyone here in Charlotte or North Carolina. I just don't know why anyone would do something like this to me, especially in front of my baby," I started to whine again.

Shelton wiped the tears away from my eyes. He kissed my fingers and then began to kiss my face.

"I love you...just don't ever do something like that again okay? I'm sorry for getting upset, it wasn't your fault. I just need to know where you are, at all times, from here on out," Shelton

said in a serious tone, but I had no
disagreements.

I concentrated on the throbbing sensation in
the back of my head.

Whoever had done this to me deserved to rot
in Hell…but for now; prison would just have
to do.

~**********~

*~Life has a way of changing for the good or for the
bad in a blink of an eye. The trick is to embrace and
face change and learn to make it work to benefit
you. Take your life for a ride…or get left behind~*

Anonymous

Chapter Three

"Dianna, you don't have to be here. I'm fine, really," I told her for the tenth time in less than an hour.

Dianna was the church Secretary; and *our* best friend.

Over the years, she and I had become fairly close; naturally so, since she and Shelton were as close as sister and brother.

He was always watching over her.

In my opinion, he was way to overprotective when it came to her.

Some, most, thought that they were having an affair; but I disagreed...most of the time.

As close as they were, to imagine them in that way; or any more than just friends...almost seemed like it would be incest or something.

For the life of me, I just couldn't visualize them being anything more than what they were.

Friends.

Willingly, they allowed me into their circle.

To be honest I had grown quite fond of her.

Dianna was a sweet as a caramel apple or a frosted cupcake with extra sprinkles.

Sorry...I'm a little hungry.

But Dianna was harmless.

She was truly like the little sister I never had.

I couldn't help myself...I absolutely adored her.

She was my friend; my therapist.

Yes, I guess giving her the title of my best friend; as well---was more than appropriate.

I had never had a best friend before, other than Mama, so I imagined that Dianna was the closest thing to it.

She was the logic behind all of my crazy ideas, and she was the shoulder that I often leaned on whenever I was feeling overwhelmed.

I hadn't had many friends in my past---no one worth holding on to; or the one's that had been somewhat of a friend...I'd accidentally ended up being more than a *friend* to their man.

As I said...I had some whorish ways.

So, Dianna had been the first woman that I had actually become close with since I changed my life.

She was the first woman, other than Mama, that I somewhat trusted.

I still only told her what I wanted her to know, because as far as I was concerned...her loyalty would always *first* lie with Shelton.

So, she knew nothing about my past...but I was willing to bet that she knew quite a bit about Shelton's...no matter how hard she tried to deny it.

"Girl, I wish you would just stop saying that already, because I'm not going anywhere. Shelton made me promise him that I would stay no matter how many times you told me to go," Dianna laughed.

Okay, so did it bother me that they were *so* close?

Sometimes.

And did I truly trust him around a young, beautiful, single woman in her twenties...

Sometimes.

But despite the talk and so called advice from the Mothers of the church, whenever I would mention anything about it to Shelton; he would only laugh.

He assured me that nothing was and never would go on between the two of them.

I believed him.

"Well, at least make yourself useful and cook me some lunch or something," I joked with her, seeing that getting rid of her was out of the question.

"Oh, Maxi, got jokes huh? Now, you know I can't cook," Dianna said, taking a seat beside of me.

Oh, yeah, that's right…she couldn't.

Yep, she didn't have a chance with Shelton.

His stomach wore the pants in this relationship; and a woman that couldn't cook-couldn't do a thing for him.

"Can I ask you something?" I said to her, scheming up a few questions.

"Shoot for it," she said nonchalantly.

"How do you really know Shelton? And I want the real answer, not the fake story that you both told me," I said to her, giving her the evil eye.

As close as they were, they had to have some *real* history; not just previous church history.

"What? What are you talking about?" Dianna asked uncomfortably.

I just looked at her, silently, patiently waiting.

"Maxi, come on. We met in church. He used to be a minister at my father's church, St. Johns, as you know; for years. Shelton was ready to branch out on his own so he transferred to take the Pastor position at New Hope. I came to visit the first Sunday that he was set to preach, spoke to him after the service, and he asked if I would stick around and be his secretary. He said he wanted someone in the position that he knew and that he could trust. He had been like a son to my father...literally; which made him *like* my brother. So, I felt that it was only right that I accept his offer," Dianna concluded.

She and Shelton always told the same, exact story…the same exact way.

It almost sounded damn near rehearsed; but still yet, it was always the same.

"Did they ever catch whoever it was that did this to you?" she questioned me, obviously changing the subject.

It had been over a two weeks since the attack, but I had only been home for a few days.

Shelton hadn't left my side, not even once, so he was far behind on church business.

I forced him to tend to his other duties, but he insisted that Dianna came over to babysit Mackenzie…and me.

"No, not yet. They said that they had a witness; but we haven't heard anything else from them," I responded.

No matter what the police thought, I was convinced that I didn't know the person who'd attacked me.

I mean, I had no enemies; hell pretty much, no one even knew that I existed.

I didn't have any family and I didn't keep in contact with anybody once I left Texas; so in my opinion, the police were wrong.

My attack couldn't have been personal.

But I was dying to know who it was.

Why on earth would someone attack a woman, with her child, for no reason at all?

People could be so cruel.

And other than that, why go through all of the trouble of knocking me out, pretty much leaving me for dead, yet they didn't touch or take a thing?

It just didn't make sense to me.

Things just weren't adding up.

But whoever it was deserved every bit of what was coming to them.

I'll admit, though I was grateful to be alive, the near death experience had me, and Shelton, both acting just a tad bit out of character.

Shelton was running around in protection mode.

I was seeing a lot more of those *street* qualities; that usually he tried to hide.

The old holy version of him, was on a little break; at least that was how it seemed.

Instead of love and hope in his eyes, lately I was seeing revenge; and just a small speck of hate.

He just seemed as though he was ready to go to war; or as if he was ready to go do a *drive by* or something.

But, despite how much he was on edge, he was still being the perfect husband; as always.

Shelton was doing everything that he could to make sure that I was comfortable; and he made sure that I felt safe.

For the most part; I felt safe.

But to be honest, I wasn't exactly sure as to what else I was feeling.

It wasn't all righteous and holy---that was for sure.

All I knew was that someone had tried to kill me...and I wanted to know why.

"Hey...you okay?" Dianna snapped at me.

Little did she know---she almost got smacked; but instead, I simply nodded and smiled.

"Well, how about I *order* us some lunch huh," Dianna said as she headed toward the kitchen.

I laughed at her behind her back.

How was she ever going to get a husband if she couldn't cook?

~***~

"Hey you, how was your day? How are you feeling?" Shelton asked me, immediately upon entering the house.

He dropped his bags by the front door, approached me and then kissed my forehead.

Before I could even answer him, he spoke to Dianna and reached for Mackenzie, who started to clap once she was in his arms.

"Thanks Dianna for helping Maxi today. I don't know what I would do without you," Shelton praised Dianna.

I looked directly at her.

Wait a minute…

Did the bit---excuse me; did she just blush?

I sure looked like a slight blush to me!

"Oh, it was no problem, really, anything for you and *my bestie*. I love you guys to pieces, bro," she joked and playfully punched him in his arm.

Her words and actions relaxed me...to a certain extent.

Maxi, get it together…

It was obvious that their relationship was innocent.

I smiled as Dianna made her way over to me. She hugged my neck, kissed my cheek, and confirmed that she was coming back tomorrow---whether I wanted her to or not.

As the front door closed behind her, I turned my attention to Shelton.

I studied him in silence.

I watched him in thought.

"Babe, how about pizza for dinner?" he asked.

I frowned and nodded behind him.

"Sorry, that's what we had for lunch. I'll cook you something, what do you want?" I asked attempting to get up from the couch.

"No, sit back down. I'll cook for you instead, okay?" Shelton said, pointing for me to retake my seat.

I knew that I didn't have much of a choice, so I sat back down, and watched him and Mackenzie head to the kitchen.

Soon, followed the opening and shutting of cabinets, pots rattling and hitting the floor.

Lord, please don't let him burn the house down!

I thought about getting up to assist, but I knew that it would only be a waste of time.

After things quieted down, I closed my eyes. Touching the back of my head, I could still feel the stitches; but for the most part, the swelling had gone down.

For some reason, I began to think about what death.

What would have happened if I'd died?

Who would have helped Shelton take care of

Mackenzie?

Would it have been Dianna?

I entertained a vision of them.

They were laughing together, and both of them

were holding one of Mackenzie's hands.

The expression on Dianna's face, for Shelton,

no longer said brotherly love; but her face was

full of passion, love...and everything else in

between.

I looked on at them from the clouds of Heaven

with envy.

They were doing just fine; they were

happy...without me.

My eyes popped open and I shook away the

thoughts and the disturbing vision in my head.

Right away, I began to pray.

The Devil was surely up to something and I

was going to stop him in his tracks before

anything got out of hand.

There was nothing there.

I was alive for a reason.

I was still here for a purpose.

Closing my eyes again, my praying turned into napping and it wasn't until the smoke detectors began to sound, that I woke up in a panic.

"Shelton!" I screamed.

He came running into the living room with Mackenzie in one arm, and a dish rag in the other.

Shelton was covered in flour from head to toe.

He looked at me, pitifully.

"Uh, are you sure that you don't want pizza again?" he asked with the grin of a failure.

I simply smiled and shook my head.

~***~

"It was a woman?" I asked.

"According to the witness's statement," the police officer stated.

"They didn't quite get a look at her face though; she was wearing face paint and sunglasses. But the witness said that she was

101
..

pretty tall; somewhere around 5' 8" or 5' 9". She was African American, and they described the skin on her hands as being that of a caramel-coffee complexion; not too light and not too dark. They found it strange that she hadn't bothered to wear any gloves during the assault. The witness also said that during her final swing, her hat fell off and they were able to see that she had long black hair; almost blending in perfectly with her all black attire. Her body frame was described as being very slender; maybe 150 pounds at the most. The attacker struck you with some kind of thick piece of wood. The witness said that he caught notice of the attack just as he was about to get into his vehicle, and he yelled in her direction. He said she didn't bother to look back, only bent down to pick up her hat and then she took off running. He rushed over to you and instead of chasing after her, he tended to your the cries of your daughter, and then called 911. I know it's a lot to take in, but I have to ask you this; is there any one that you know, that might fit the woman's description?" the policeman asked.

Hell yes…and I was looking right at her.

Dianna appeared in the doorway of my bedroom.

Everything single detail…described Dianna.

Down to the tee.

And I do mean down to the very last detail.

She was that exact height.

Damn near that same complexion.

She was pretty much that exact weight and her hair was long and black, and rested in the middle of her back.

"Mrs. Cartwright, are you still there?" I heard the police officer ask.

"Yes, I'm here. I'll get back to you," I said and hung up before he had a chance to respond.

I looked at Dianna from head to toe.

Of all people…it was her?

Why would she try to kill me?

I mentally criticized myself for even pondering that question.

It was the obvious why she had done it; she wanted my life...she wanted my husband.

"Everything okay boo?" Dianna asked me, being her usual perky self.

And to think that I really considered her to be my friend; I should have known.

I had never been trustworthy in my past friendships...maybe this was some type of karma.

But I'd changed, I really had.

Didn't that count for something?

My biggest question was how had Dianna known that I was going to Charlotte that day?

Had she been sitting somewhere in the cut when I left?

Had she followed me all the way there?

Had she watched me the whole time; waiting for the perfect opportunity to strike?

There were so many unanswered questions.

There were so many things that I just didn't understand.

She was supposed to be my best friend.

"Bitch...get...out," I said in a voice that may have given her the impression that I was calm; but for her sake, she sure as hell had better seen it as a warning.

She gasped and covered her mouth.

Yes; you damn right I said *bitch*; and I meant it too!

At that moment, I didn't give two rats asses about what she or anyone else thought about my choice of words!

I wasn't in the mood to uphold my perfect Pastor's wife image!

"Max---" Dianna started to say.

"You heard what I said...get out!" I screamed and stood up from the edge of my bed.

I'd never seen anyone move so fast in all of my life!

Mackenzie started to cry from the sudden loudness of my voice but I ignored her and headed to the bedroom window.

Dianna had just reached her car and it looked as though she was on her cell phone.

Of course she was calling Shelton.

She drove off and my next guess was that any minute now, Shelton would be arriving at home.

I was right.

In a matter of minutes, Shelton pulled into the drive way and came running toward the house.

I grabbed my daughter and made my way into the living room.

When Shelton entered, he halted at the sight of me and took only a second to catch his breath.

"Maxi, what's wrong honey? What's wrong?" was all he asked.

I was surprised.

I actually expected him to come in fussing about my use of words and demanding an explanation for putting Dianna out of the house; but he didn't.

I didn't respond, I just stared at him.

I was looking for something but I wasn't quite sure what.

Had he had something to do with this?

Did he and Dianna have some type of plan to get rid of me?

"Baby, say something, talk to me, what's wrong?" he asked again, now sitting on the couch beside of me, taking Mackenzie from my arms.

"The police called. The witness described my attacker...they described Dianna," I said still in disbelief.

At first, Shelton looked confused.

For only about a second; he looked shocked.

But that didn't last long.

Right before my very eyes, Shelton *evicted* shock and confusion; and anger and hatred signed the *lease* and moved right on in!

The fury fires of Hell were visible in Shelton's eyes and I simply couldn't put into words what was written all over his face.

And for the first time, ever...he didn't try to hide it.

~**********~

~Sometimes, the only person worth

trusting...entirely...is you~

Anonymous

Chapter Four

Though my body was sitting in church, my mind was everywhere else.

I was wondering about Dianna.

After I told Shelton what the police officer said about my attacker, he called Dianna and had her come back to the house.

She, as always, had done exactly what Shelton had asked her to; but I don't think even she expected or was prepared to Shelton's actions and behavior.

I know I sure as hell wasn't.

Shelton was hollering and screaming, throwing things, and demanding answers that she pretended not to have.

He broke a lamp, punched a hole in the wall, and even gave Dianna a little shove.

It was clear that he wanted to hurt her...and I mean real, real bad.

He was scaring the crap out of all of us.

Still, no matter what he said, or done, Dianna denied any involvement in my attack.

She cried more than she spoke and said that she would never do anything to hurt me. Although all odds were against her and the witness had described her at the scene of the crime, in a way...I felt as though she was telling the truth.

But Shelton wasn't buying it.

He went on and on about how no one was going to take his wife away from him and a whole bunch of other bull crap that no one understood but him.

Finally after a whole hour of fussing, swearing, and everything else that you could think of, Shelton kicked Dianna out of our house; and out of the church.

He told her that he never wanted to see or hear from her again---and we both knew that he meant it.

She ran out of our house that day, with her head in her hands, crying like she'd just lost her best friend…technically, she had; we all had.

After Shelton and I sat in front of each other for quite some time, not saying a word, finally he was the first to break his silence.

He said that we had to forgive her whether we wanted to or not and that she would have to answer to God for what she had done.

Okay, the Pastor was back.

We agreed that we weren't going to call the police.

If they tracked her down, good; if they didn't, she would just have to live every day of the rest of her life, knowing what she had done to me.

The truth to the matter was pretty simple; despite what she had done…we both loved her.

If I felt angry, and betrayed; I could only imagine what Shelton was feeling.

No matter what, I just couldn't believe that Dianna had tried to kill me.

God, why did it have to be her?

I trusted her.

I loved her.

And now I felt so stupid.

I should have listened to everyone and everything that was said about her.

I guess that's what I get for not listening to my elders.

The Mothers could see it; but I couldn't...or maybe it was that I wouldn't.

Nevertheless, it was clear.

I mean, what other reason would Dianna attack me, unless it was because she was in love with my husband?

For hours that day, I watched Shelton as he paced back and forth.

He was sweating, and mumbling to himself, as though he too, was trying to figure it all out.

He even ignored the cries of Mackenzie; which was something he'd never done before.

Without saying a word, he started to clean up the mess that he had made.

I personally couldn't believe that he had allowed himself to get as upset as he did.

But one thing was for sure; I had been right about his *secret* temper and anger problem.

Shelton showed his ass that day; and now that I knew what he was capable of...I surely wouldn't be pissing him off anytime soon.

That same night, I overheard him crying in the bathroom as he pretended to be in the shower.

I stood by the door; silently crying right along with him.

Shelton's cries pierced my soul, and I knew that Dianna's actions had hurt him to the core.

He was heartbroken...we both were.

But no matter what; what Dianna had done would never be forgotten.

No matter how bad we both wanted to pretend that it never happened.

The church, in unison, said *Amen*, and I redirected my attention back to Shelton and the sermon.

Rightfully so, this Sunday, Shelton was preaching about forgiveness.

He spoke about how forgiveness wasn't necessarily about the other person; but more or less, it was about you.

It was for your own sake.

He reminded the congregation that no one was perfect and that all people sin and fall short of the glory of God.

But you must love them anyway and continue to pray for them.

Shelton even mentioned the part about if someone has wronged you, or if you have wronged anyone; that the Bible says that you should go and ask them for their forgiveness.

Shelton's eyes were on me the entire time that he spoke...as though in a way he was asking for me for my forgiveness.

What was he sorry about?

Shelton's natural glow was gone.

He looked so sad...or maybe he looked tired.

Either way; he was definitely not himself.

..

If I could see it...I was sure that everyone else could see it too.

Still yet, his preaching was still on point; just like it always was.

Church was over, and everyone mingled and talked with one another as if they didn't have a care in the world.

More so than usual, I remained to myself.

I wasn't really in much of a talking mood.

Shelton hugged me as soon as he stepped down from the pulpit.

It was a different kind of hug; long and lingering.

As though his body was trying to tell me something, that his mouth just couldn't say.

After he released me, he continued on, greeting and speaking to the members and the guests.

Next, I handed off Mackenzie to one of the Mothers of the church, and headed to the bathroom.

Washing my face in cold water, I tried to collect my thoughts.

I was all in my feelings and I just couldn't seem to pull myself together.

I felt like crying.

I felt like screaming.

And in a metaphorical kind of way; I felt like dying.

But I was sure that one way or the other, it wouldn't solve anything.

Nothing could ease the pain that was in my heart.

For more reasons than I could begin to explain, I felt empty; I felt defeated.

It was times like this that I needed Mama's advice and encouragement.

Lord knows I needed her.

She always had something positive to say.

She could always see the best out of a bad situation.

I just needed to know what to do.

I was feeling so strange; and not to mention that Shelton was still acting unusual.

He was still not quite his normal self.

Lately, he hadn't said much; all he had done was pray.

Whether it was at home, or at the church, he was always praying.

He'd apologized to me for his behavior and for losing his temper, but I'd always known that he had it in him.

I guess trying to kill a man's wife was enough to bring it out of anyone; even a man of God.

Checking my appearance once more in the bathroom mirror, I fixed my dress, and I turned around to head out the door.

But I was stopped dead in my tracks...

Dianna.

She looked at me; looking at her.

She was teary eyed, and she looked as though she hadn't slept in a week.

There were so many mixed emotions running around inside of me all at once.

My mind was in so much of a whirlwind that I almost lost my balance.

I was unsure of what to say or what to do; or which one of my feelings to act on first.

Luckily, I didn't have to.

"I didn't do it. I swear it wasn't me," Dianna said as she went running out of the bathroom.

I wanted to chase after her but I couldn't lift my feet off of the ground.

My thoughts were all over the place.

Why *did* I believe her?

But if *she* didn't do it...then who did?

After a few more minutes, I was finally able to head back into the sanctuary.

I spotted Mackenzie being loved on and passed around from person to person, and then I spotted Shelton.

He was talking to someone at the back of the church.

Their backs were toward me, but from a distance, I would have thought that it was Dianna...only Dianna had been wearing a green dress.

This woman was wearing a red.

I waited for them to turn around but they never did.

Just as I headed in their direction, the woman proceeded with walking out of the church doors, and then and only then, did Shelton turn around.

He scanned the crowd as though he was looking for me, and when he found me, he smiled.

I ignored him and didn't return the gesture.

Lord...who was that woman?

~***~

"Dianna came by the church last Sunday, did you see her?" I asked Shelton as I rubbed his back.

We hadn't exactly had too much time to talk here lately.

Tonight had been the first night that Shelton had actually come home at a decent time, and with Mackenzie already asleep, we had some time to ourselves.

Shelton turned over to look at me, and I motioned for him to lie back down on his stomach.

"What? When?" He asked concerned.

"She came into the bathroom. She was crying and she said that she didn't do it; that she didn't attack me. And call me crazy, but you know what? I think I believe her," I said calmly.

"You do?" Shelton questioned.

In all honesty, I did.

Maybe the witness made a mistake.

"I think so. You didn't see her? You were right near the door talking to that lady; she had to have run right by you," I proclaimed, intentionally bringing up the woman.

"No, I didn't see her; I must have been talking to a visitor...most likely the woman that wore the red dress. She went on and on about how much she enjoyed the service and planned to come back this Sunday. She had quite a few questions about forgiveness. And you know me; I get so caught up in talking about the Lord, that Dianna probably slipped right pass me," Shelton stated in a somewhat exhausted tone.

With his voluntarily explanation about the woman, I concluded that there was nothing to worry about, so I felt there was no need to carry on the conversation.

Maybe we could do something that required a little *less* talking.

It had been a while since my husband had touched me in *that* way.

We hadn't been intimate since the day before my attack, and that was pushing over a month ago.

I kissed Shelton's back and then continued to rub his shoulders.

He didn't say anything nor did he move, so I did it again.

Nothing.

I stopped rubbing and headed toward his ear and guess what…he snores.

"Shelton?" I called his name, but his snoring answered my call.

Maybe he really was tired.

Disappointed, I headed to the bathroom to take a shower.

As I showered, I made up in my mind that I was going to call Dianna the next day.

I figured that I would do just as Shelton had preached...forgive her, and actually get her side of the story.

With all the yelling and fussing that Shelton had done, she had barely been able to say a full sentence, so I wanted to give her a chance.

No, we would never be best friends or even friends again; but at least I could hear her out.

Since that day, we hadn't heard from the police, and at this point, I was just ready to forget about the whole thing and move on.

I was okay, my family was okay, and really, that was all that truly mattered.

The soothing, warm water, washed away all of my worries and concerns.

For the first time in what seemed like such a long time, for some reason; I smiled.

God's presence suddenly came over me and I felt nothing but peace.

Yes, everything was going to be just fine.

I got out of the shower, and didn't bother to dry off.

Cutting off the bathroom light, I stepped into the bedroom.

I was just a little startled as I looked up and saw Shelton, sitting on the edge of the bed.

The room, now, smelled somewhat fruity.

There was music playing, softly, and rose petals all over the bed and the floor.

Shelton must have forgotten where I kept the candles, because he had taken the ones from the living room, lit them, and placed them in different spots around the room.

He fooled me; in a good way.

"Do you think it would be alright if I made love to my wife tonight?" Shelton asked me.

For some reason, tears began to fall from my eyes as I nodded.

God, I love this man.

I just wanted to spend the rest of my life with him.

If I could have nothing else, that would be more than enough for me.

Shelton picked up my wet body and carried me to the bed.

And for the first time, since the night of our honeymoon, Shelton took his time with me.

He loved on me, caressed me, and didn't dirty talk; not even once.

For the first time in a long time, he made love to me...like a Pastor.

The next morning, I decided to make him breakfast in bed.

It had been a while, especially since we had Mackenzie, that I had done little things like that for him.

He enjoyed and appreciated it so much, that he said that he was spending the entire day with his family.

No church business, no running here and there; it would just be us.

I was so excited that I found a hundred things for us to do but Shelton didn't really mind.

We got out and about, did some shopping, and spent some much needed quality time together.

A little laughing and some bonding, was just what we both needed.

Shelton even got to see Mackenzie get her ears pierced.

After lunch, we decided to stop for ice cream and then head to the park.

It wasn't unbearably hot, so it was the perfect day for a stroll around the lake, and to feed the ducks.

All was well.

All was fine; at least for a little while.

"Pastor Shelton?"

We both turned around to face the man
blocking the sunlight.

He was a big, bald, chocolate black man, with
enough muscles to have been a steroids
spokesperson.

"What a surprise," Shelton responded and
extended his hand.

"How are you doing pretty lady? I'm an old
buddy of your husband's...John," the man said
and reached out his hand in my direction.

John---the man from the phone that day.

I shook his hand and gave him a fake grin.

He called himself a friend; apparently, he and
Shelton weren't on the same page about the
whole friendship thing.

For a while, Shelton and John, small talked and
then Shelton asked me to give him a second
and he and the strange man walked off.

They walked far enough away to where I
couldn't hear what they were saying.

I had a funny feeling about this man.

Something about him made me feel like he couldn't be trusted.

Taking a seat on the bench, I handed Mackenzie the remainder of her ice cream and searched my purse for my phone.

Glancing at Shelton and whoever *he* really was once more, I figured that now was as good as a time as any to call Dianna.

I called her twice but she didn't pick up her cell; so I called her house.

No answer.

Not thinking much of it, I sent her a text asking her to call me as soon as she could.

I waited on her response, but it never came.

You would think that she would be interested in seeing what I had to say.

Unless...

Maybe reaching out to her wasn't such a good idea.

Impatiently, I waited on Shelton to finish his private conversation.

Finally, the *John* walked away and Shelton headed back toward us.

"Come on honey, let's go," he said in a low voice.

"Huh…why?" I questioned him.

"Because I said so, that's why. Look I'm sorry, let's just go, okay?" Shelton asked the question, though he really didn't care for my answer.

All of a sudden his mood had changed and I was sure that it had something to do with that man.

I didn't know who he was, but I was surely going to make it my business to find out.

~***~

Shelton stayed home with Mackenzie while I ran to the grocery store.

I rushed in to get everything that I needed so that I could have a few extra minutes to make a quick stop.

I was going by Dianna's house.

It had been over a week since I had called her, but she still hadn't gotten back to me.

I really wanted to give her a chance; to hear her out.

But more importantly; I wanted to know if she knew anything about *John*.

Trust me, if anyone knew who *John* was...she did.

That day after leaving the park, Shelton explained that once upon a time they could have been considered as friends, maybe.

But that John just a one of the many people that he chose to leave behind once he decided to fully dedicate his life to God.

I took his explanation for what it was, but I wasn't stupid---it was more to that story.

I was sure that Shelton had no real plans on sharing the whole truth about their relationship, but I didn't need him to.

I would find out all by myself; all on my own.

Arriving at Dianna's house, I discovered that it was no longer *her* house.

There was a For Rent sign in the yard.

She moved?

When?

Where?

Why?

Why would Dianna pick up and move?

She loved this house!

Realizing that it was about time to start making
it back home before Shelton started to worry, I
drove speedily away, all the while attempting
to sort out my thoughts.

I wondered where Dianna had gone.

Where had she moved?

Was she still here in South Carolina?

Or was she gone?

Dianna had always loved her home.

Though she was only renting, being a single
woman, living all alone, she'd always said that
there, in that house and in that neighborhood,
she felt safe.

I couldn't imagine why she would move
anywhere else; unless she moved *somewhere*
else; maybe even far, far away.

She was running from something.

Either Dianna was running because she was guilty; or she was running because she was innocent---and we, Shelton and I, had insulted and hurt her so much from our accusations, that she felt the only thing left to do was to go. Either way, I wanted to find her; I needed to find her.

I just wanted to talk to her.

Just as I pulled into the drive way, Shelton was calling my cell phone.

I must have been gone a few minutes too long.

He had been extremely clingy lately.

He was even worse than he had been after my attack.

He was coming home early from the church.

He wasn't staying gone all day without calling.

Actually, Shelton was calling darn near every chance that he got.

When I asked him if there was anything to be concerned about, he simply said that it was just time for him to get his priorities in order.

God and family were his top priorities.

Hey...I couldn't argue with that.

That night, Dianna was the star of the show in my dreams.

I dreamed of her crying and driving down a highway with a car full of her belongings. In my dreams she was doing the exact same thing that I had done when I left my past behind in Texas.

The whole dream, she kept repeating over and over that she didn't do it.

Though I was the victim, I felt so sorry for her. Even though I didn't want to...I did.

The next morning, as soon as I opened my eyes, I tried calling her again, but she still didn't answer.

Then, I decided to call the Charlotte police just to see if there was anything new; any leads or more information from the witness.

But there wasn't.

Just to be sure, I asked them to double check with the witness to make sure that he described the woman to the best of his ability. They promised that they would give it another shot.

It was worth another try.

I made sure that I told Shelton that I was going into town later on that day.

I told him that I was going to the Farmers Market and to a few other places; but I lied.

Really, I was going to Dianna's fathers' church; Shelton's home church...

St. John Missionary Baptist Church.

I was going to ask him if he had seen or heard from Dianna.

It was a Friday; but if he was anything like Shelton, I was sure that he was at the church.

After all, he had been Shelton's mentor for years, and I could only assumed that Shelton was only following his actions; or at least doing what he had been shown that Pastor's do.

Pulling up in front of the church, I could see that God was truly in the blessing business.

The church was breathtakingly beautiful.

I hadn't seen it in about two years, but it definitely wasn't the same old church that used to sit on that corner.

It had been remodeled and it looked absolutely amazing.

Though I'd been by it a few times, I had never been inside.

Since this church was Baptist and our church was Non-Denominational, we didn't fellowship as much as we probably should have.

And Shelton had never mentioned going back to visit; nor had Dianna's father Bishop Clarence Forney, ever come to see Shelton in action.

I always found that strange, but I tried my best to stay out of *Pastor* related business.

But if I had to guess; I was putting my money on the fact that the Bishop probably wasn't exactly too happy with Shelton's sudden departure...or that Shelton took Dianna with him.

Walking through the church doors, the inside was just as stunning as the outside.

It was as if they were trying to get as close to looking like Heaven as they possibly could. Everything was so grand; white and gold.

"Hello, can I help you?" a scruffy voice said from behind me.

"Oh hi, I'm looking for Bishop Clarence," I said, genuinely smiling at the older gentleman.

"Well you've found him, how can I help you young lady?" he asked shaking my hand.

"Well, I'm Shelton's wife, Maxine, and I was wondering if you had seen or heard from your daughter...Dianna? I tried calling her but she hasn't returned my calls. I went by her place also, but she has moved," I told him.

"Who? Darling maybe you are mistaken. I don't have a daughter named Dianna," he said as a matter of fact.

Huh?

"You are Bishop Clarence Forney right? I was told that Dianna Forney was your daughter?" I said hoping that he misunderstood me the first time.

"Yes, I'm Bishop Clarence Forney; but I can assure you that I don't have a daughter named Dianna, to be exact, I don't have a daughter at all...only three sons," he continued to explain.

What?

What in the hell is going on here?

"Would you happen to have a son named Shelton?" I asked fishing for answers but he shook his head.

"Nope, I don't know anyone by the name of Shelton either. I'm sorry you must have the wrong Bishop...and the wrong church," he said, and bid me goodbye.

No, it was indeed the right church...

I knew that for a fact.

But there was something fishy going on around here...and I was going to find out what it was!

I stormed out of the church on fire!

I was so upset that I couldn't think straight.

Unable to force myself to drive off, I sat there

for a second to think about what I'd just heard.

You mean to tell me that both of them had

been lying to me the whole time?

I guess a part of me had always known it.

I had been right about their little story all

along.

So now, there was only one simple question.

Who are they?

~**********~

~If you wait long enough, you will see, find, or
receive everything that you have always been meant
to have. The failure comes in when you rush
something...that just wasn't quite ready~

Anonymous

Chapter Five

A few weeks had gone by since I had found
out that Shelton and Dianna had been lying
about their entire relationship and the way
they'd met.

I'd always known in the back of my mind that
they were feeding me bull---but never, never
had I thought that it would have been
something like this.

I mean the lie was a bit extreme.

Bishop Clarence had never even heard of
Dianna, or Shelton, so that means that they had
some type of past together---that they both
were trying to hide.

They had been covering up something the
whole time.

Though it was eating me up inside, I decided
not to mention my little visit to St. John or my
conversation with the Bishop to Shelton; at
least not until I had done my own
investigation.

But one thing was for sure, and that was if Shelton had told one lie---he'd probably told many others.

That's just the way that *lying* worked.

And though I had my own lies and secrets; to find out that Shelton had a few of his own; just left a bad taste in my mouth.

I was now questioning everything that Shelton had ever told me.

He was a Pastor; he just wasn't supposed to tell lies!

Hell, if you couldn't believe a Pastor...then who could you believe?

In my opinion; if you couldn't trust a Pastor...you couldn't trust anyone.

"When will you be home?" I asked Shelton as I sat down in front of the computer.

"I'll be home before the sun goes down, unless you need me to come home now," he responded sincerely.

"No, I'm fine. I'll see you later," I said, and then we said our goodbyes.

Smiling at Mackenzie destroying the kitchen floor with her toys, I typed in Shelton's full name on a particular site on the web and what do you know…nothing.

At least there was nothing in South Carolina; older than five or six years for him.

There was no record of his birth, nothing matching his name and birthday.

It was just as if he'd popped up out of nowhere.

There were a few men with his exact same name and birthday but they were all showing pretty old in age, a million miles away…or dead.

Basically, there was no way that Shelton Cartwright was my husband's real name.

My heart skipped a beat and I desperately tried to calm myself down.

I steadied my breathing and tried to think.

Okay, logically, I guess maybe with him being an orphan and all; maybe his name had been changed.

It was definitely a possibility and it would most certainly explain things.

That is, if he was ever really an orphan at all.

Hmm…who was I married to?

I sure as hell didn't have a clue.

Next, I searched Dianna Forney.

And just like Shelton…nothing for her either; that was older than five years.

I double checked Bishop's story by searching him as well.

There was plenty of information on him, his church, his wife…and his three sons.

But just as he'd said; there was no daughter…no Dianna Forney.

It was as if neither of them actually existed.

I was as hot as hen piss!

I got up from the computer and headed to my secret stash for a glass, scratch that…the whole bottle of wine.

What in the hell was going on around here?

~***~

I lied to Shelton about not feeling well enough to attend church.

Will the lying ever stop?

Eventually.

Maybe.

The truth was, I had lost all respect for Shelton in a sense; and I didn't want to listen to him preach.

He was a liar, and even though I wasn't the most honest person, at least I wasn't calling myself a Pastor and preaching from a pulpit every Sunday morning.

I was just a side kick.

Shelton didn't press the issue, and he and Mackenzie, headed to the church, leaving me behind.

If only there was someone that I could talk to, to help me come up with a whole bunch of maybe's or possibilities and alternates to the truth; but I had no one---no one at all.

I just needed some answers to my questions.

There were so many things that I wanted to say but I couldn't, or maybe it was that I shouldn't...so I didn't.

As I attempted to sort out my thoughts and feelings, Shelton's phone on his side of the bed, began to vibrate.

He was going to have a fit when he figured out that he left it behind.

He never went anywhere without his phone.

Before I could pick it up, the vibration stopped.

I checked the call log and found that it was from a Private Number.

Scrolling down the list, there were numerous of Private calls; some missed...and some answered.

I held the phone, hoping that it would vibrate again, but of course it didn't.

Who on earth would be calling him from a Private number?

Ugh...and the mystery continues.

Sadly, I was starting to feel like I was married to a complete stranger.

I'd always suspected that he may have had a few things in his past that he'd failed to mention; but who knew that he had a whole damn list!

Shelton had a closet full of secrets that little by little, were starting to surface.

All this time I wanted to know everything about Shelton and his past, and now...I wasn't so sure.

Thoughts of Shelton and Dianna were running wild in my head.

Who were they...really?

Where did they come from?

Maybe they used to be lovers.

That was definitely a possibility.

Just thinking about it made my skin crawl.

No, it just couldn't be that.

Maybe they knew each other from his days as an orphan.

But then why would they lie about it?

Why would they lie about...everything?

About her being a Pastor's daughter or about him ministering at the church she grew up in…everything?

I should have known that there was something else between them but I tried to give them the benefit of the doubt.

I tried to avoid the rumors.

I tried to believe whatever Shelton told me to believe because he was a saint…and not a sinner.

He preached every Wednesday night and Sunday morning.

He did everything by the *good book*.

He obeyed all of the Ten Commandments; so that meant that he couldn't and wouldn't lie to me---at least that's what I'd thought.

So the real question was…now what?

Do I tell him that I know he isn't who he says that he is?

Do I confront him about his lies or about Dianna, and St. Johns?

Or, do I just keep my mouth shut and continue living my life; a life with a husband who loves me and has never done anything to hurt me, at least not that *he* knows of?

If I called him out on his lies, it was only fair that I be honest with him about my own.

But was that something that I really wanted to do?

Was that something that I was really ready to do?

But from the looks of it...my lies were nothing compared to his.

Shelton hadn't been the first man that I'd lied to.

I'd never been completely honest with *any* man, in my entire life.

Considering what I found out once Mama died about her lies about my Daddy; just maybe I inherited that horrible trait...along with these *god* awful, child baring hips.

For the most part, I lied because I hated to be judged.

I hated for someone not to agree with my choices, so, I'd always thought that the solution to it all was fairly simple…lie.

But on the flip side…I hated to be lied to.

It may sound a bit stupid, but it was the truth.

My truth at least.

I wanted more honesty than I was willing to give in return.

Mama would always say: Only do or say what you would want someone to do or say to you.

Let's just say…Mama had a lot of advice that I failed to take…and evidently, she hadn't taken all of it herself.

But at that moment, I made up my mind that it was time for the lying to stop.

It was time for both of us to come clean; about everything.

If we had any real chance of making our marriage work, it was time to start telling the truth.

Concluding my thoughts, finally I rolled out of bed, and headed to the bathroom but something just didn't feel right.

I paused for a second to see if my head would stop spinning, but standing still only appeared to make it worse.

Just as I took my next step, my mouth started to water and I ran to the bathroom, barely making it to the toilet to throw up.

Uh oh.

~***~

"I hope it's a boy! I've always wanted a son," Shelton squealed, rubbing my stomach.

That's right, I was pregnant---and damn it, I wasn't happy about it!

A baby?

Right Now?

This was the worst thing that could have happened to me!

We weren't in exactly the best position to be having another child; whether Shelton knew it or not.

Our marriage wasn't exactly on stable ground, and a baby just made everything complicated. Being pregnant still hadn't changed the facts; but it had definitely painted a different picture. I found out that I was six weeks pregnant, that same Sunday I missed church; at the hospital later on that evening.

Shelton and I never got the chance to have our much needed conversation.

Since the news, I was skeptical about laying all of our cards on the table.

What if he wanted to leave me because I wasn't as *pure* as he'd thought I'd been?

And being married before...that was surely a deal breaker or at least enough to make him feel deceived.

What if he asked for a divorce?

Could I really do that to myself...and to my kids?

I had grown up without a father and I refused to do that to my own children.

A single parent home just wasn't an option.

Still yet, keeping quiet also meant that I would never know the truth about Shelton.

I would never know who he really was or where he had really come from.

Most likely, I would never know how he and Dianna really knew each other.

And of all the things; that bothered me the most.

So, for now, the only choice I had was to pretend as though everything was okay.

"Well, you know if it is a boy...we're done. No more babies mister," I said in a serious tone.

"What are you talking about? I told you that I wanted a big family woman. Now if you tricked me into marrying you, the jokes on you. You owe me at least two more kids after this one," Shelton joked.

I... tricked... him?

What a choice of words.

"Have you heard from Dianna---at all, since that day? I tried calling her, but I didn't get an answer," I asked deliberately changing the subject.

Shelton was silent for only a moment.

"No, I haven't," he responded nonchalantly, and started to kiss my lips.

It was obvious that he didn't want to talk about her, so I said nothing else about her.

I allowed Shelton to have his way with me, but my mind definitely wasn't on the sex.

And believe me…that was a first.

As always, once he was done, he was out cold.

After he began to snore, I got up from the bed and sat in the chair beside the window.

Everything was so quiet and still; all except for the sound of crickets.

Staring up at the moon, I admired its beauty as I thought about my life.

The saying, if it ain't broke...don't fix it, for some reason kept popping in and out of my head.

Life had a way of pulling you in so many different directions, all at once.

You could only hope to choose the right path.

Lost in my thoughts, I almost missed it, but something forced me to pay attention.

Shelton was sleep talking...again.

Shelton talked in his sleep often; usually about nothing in particular, but as I paid close attention to the words that were coming out of his mouth, this time, it didn't sound too much like nonsense.

I'm sorry Maxi, please forgive me.

Shelton mumbled in his sleep.

I remained quiet.

I never meant to hurt you. I'm so sorry.

It wasn't supposed to happen.

Shelton continued to mumble away.

Oh God, was he about to say something, something that I needed to hear?

Is this some type of confession?

I moved from the chair and sat on the edge of the bed.

I waited for Shelton to say something else...but he didn't.

He never meant for what to happen?

~***~

"Do you feel well enough to go to service today?" Shelton asked me concerned.

This baby was putting it on me!

It was definitely kicking my butt!

The morning, noon and night sickness was truly taking a toll on my body.

I was tired...so, so tired.

The pregnancy was literally draining the life out of me.

This baby was making me miserable.

"Yes, I'll be there...late, but I'll be there," I said attempting to get out of bed.

Shelton helped me to my feet and stared at me as I made my way to the bathroom.

"Maybe you should stay home," he suggested now standing in the door way with Mackenzie.

I didn't say a word; I only waved him off.

I couldn't wait for all of this to be over.

Once Shelton and Mackenzie were out of sight and out of my way, slowly, I pulled myself together and headed to the church.

I listened to the whole sermon from one of the sitting rooms in the back of the church.

After it was over, and after I puked for the tenth time, I headed into the sanctuary.

"Hey, I didn't know that you were here. I thought you changed your mind and stayed home," Shelton smiled at me.

He tried to kiss me but I shook my head and grabbed my stomach, giving him a heads up that my breath may not smell the best.

Getting the hint, he frowned at me and then headed over to a few of the other members.

The Mothers surrounded me, and started giving me advice and remedies to make the pregnancy a little easier to deal with.

After a while, I tuned them out and my eyes wandered to the back of the church.

There she is…Dianna!

No…wait a minute.

That's not her...is it?

I stared at the lady at the back of the church wearing a bright red dress.

After focusing on her for just a while longer, I realized that it wasn't Dianna.

But she looked a hell of a lot like her.

She was just as tall as Dianna was.

She was even the same golden brown.

But she wasn't as pretty as Dianna.

She looked like her, sure, but a somewhat older version of her.

I stared a little longer and then it hit me.

Was she the same woman that was talking to Shelton a few weeks ago?

Was that the visitor; wearing what looked like the same exact red dress...the one with the questions about forgiveness?

Yes...that was her.

I'd only seen the back of her that time, but I was sure that it was her.

Shelton walked away from her in a hurry.

She stared at him as he walked away.

Her attention turned to me, and when she saw that I was already looking her way, hastily, she turned her head and headed out of the church. Just before crossing the threshold, she put on a pair of sunglasses.

Sunglasses…

Wait a minute…

Had she been the woman that had tried to kill me?

I could see how she could have easily been mistaken for Dianna.

I mean, they did look a hell of a lot alike.

Then it hit me.

Oh my God…

Dianna had been telling the truth!

She was innocent; Dianna was innocent.

But who was this random, almost clone of a woman…and why had she attacked me in the first place?

I didn't know…but I was going to find out!

And I was going to find out right now!

I headed toward the glass doors and the red exit sign, but Shelton stopped me mid stride.

"Maxi, what's wrong? Are you okay? Are you sick again?" Shelton asked, studying my face.

Yep, I was sick alright…sick and tired of not knowing what the hell was going on around here!

"No, I'm fine, I just need some fresh air," I lied…again.

Shelton released my arm and allowed me to continue on my journey.

Once outside, I looked around; but the lady in the red dress was nowhere in sight.

Damn it!

I tried to guess which car was hers at the stoplight down the street, but figured that it was no use.

Already outside, I decided that I may as well head across the street to the parking lot, get into my car and just go ahead home.

I was feeling nauseous again anyway, and I was much more comfortable vomiting at home, over my own toilet; where *fewer asses* had been.

Slowly walking, I was in deep thought and I felt terrible about accusing Dianna of trying to kill me.

Thinking back to that day, she was pleading for us to listen to her, but we wouldn't.

Now, I couldn't even find her to tell her that I was sorry.

Although because of the accusation, I had discovered that indeed she *was* being dishonest about some things.... so maybe an apology wasn't exactly necessary.

And this woman, whoever she was, why had she tried to hurt me?

What had I ever done to her?

Hell, I didn't even know who she was!

She had to be the one that the witness identified.

Was that why she was asking Shelton so many questions about forgiveness...out of guilt?

I was so confused.

Shaking my head, I looked in the direction of my car and hit the alarm.

I was almost across the street and then…

"No! Maxi! No!"

Everything after that was pretty much a blur.

Tires screeched as my body hit the pavement.

Face down; I could hear the sound of the car speeding away.

It wasn't until I heard screaming that I was actually able to force myself to lift my head.

From the ground, I looked behind me.

Dianna…

Where in the hell had she come from?

"Dianna!" I struggled to call out to her, but she didn't answer.

She laid there, still, in the middle of the road.

Dianna was dead.

She was dead…and she had died to save me.

Immediately, I began to cry and then I started to scream.

A flood of people spilled out of the church as I looked around for the speeding car, but it was nowhere in sight.

Dianna's eyes were open, looking in my direction...but they were lifeless; just like her unmoving body.

I squeezed my eyes shut tight and cried like I never had before.

She was gone.

She was really gone.

As soon as I opened my eyes again, I spotted Shelton in the distance, running toward me.

But he was too late.

The damage was already done.

Dianna was dead.

And looking at the blood in between my thighs...so was our unborn baby.

~**********~

~Live everyday as though it's your last; after all, it

just may be~

Anonymous

Chapter Six

The rain was making such a fuss that it was
impossible for me to sleep.

Though Shelton was still, with his back toward
me, I was sure that he was wide awake.

It had been three days since the death of
Dianna and our unborn child; and Shelton was
taking it all pretty hard.

I wasn't sure if he was sadder about losing the
baby...or if he was more hurt by the death of
Dianna.

Either way; Shelton was a total wreck.

He wasn't talking.

He wasn't eating.

And he wasn't trying to hide his emotions.

He cried frequently; especially when he would
rub my empty, lifeless stomach.

It was hard for me to see him in such a mess.

Watching him, reminded me of the agony that
I'd felt when I lost Mama.

So, I could more than imagine how he felt.

I couldn't say that I was as bad off as Shelton---
but I wasn't too far away from it.

I was full of all types of emotions that I didn't
understand.

I was sad, confused; sometimes I even felt
guilty.

It was my fault that Dianna was dead.

It was my fault that our baby was gone.

At least that's how I felt.

The reports said that the car was trying to stop
abruptly on brakes, according to the marks on
the road, but I was sure that wasn't the case.

Whoever was behind that wheel, was trying to
hit me---trying to kill me.

For what reason, I'm not sure; but I was sure
that it wasn't an accident.

Had not Dianna been somewhere looking on, I
would've been dead and gone.

Dianna.

I found it strange that Dianna had been there
all along.

She had been somewhere waiting, hiding outside the church.

I wondered what she was doing there, or why she had been there looking on in the first place. I also wondered where she had been, and why she hadn't returned any of my calls.

And most importantly...why had she chosen to spare her own life, in order to save mine?

Had she truly loved me enough, valued the friendship we once shared enough, to jump in front of a speeding car and save me?

Apparently so.

Naturally, thinking about Dianna, caused me to wonder about the lady in the red dress.

She had looked so much like her.

As far as I'd known, Dianna said that she didn't have any siblings; but then again, since she'd lied about who her father really was, there was no telling what else she had lied about.

But whether they were possibly related or not, the fact of the matter was, she was damn near identical to Dianna.

Had the woman in red been my attacker at the mall?

Had she been the woman behind the wheel? No one had gotten a good look at the car except for Dianna, and a dead witness was no witness at all.

I'd glanced at the car for only a split second before Dianna pushed me out of the way, but for the life of me, I couldn't remember what color it was.

I was in shock…but I'm not so sure that I could say the same about Dianna.

It had been something about the way that she'd yelled.

There was something in her voice; as if she'd known what was about to happen.

Like maybe she had saw it the whole time and at the last minute, she decided to take action.

Remembering the sound of her voice was the main reason why I was convinced that it wasn't an accident, or by mistake.

And no one could tell me otherwise.

Someone wanted me dead...but who and why?

As far as the baby was concerned, I was saddened, but I wasn't nearly as disappointed about the miscarriage as Shelton.

I know it sounds bad...but I couldn't help the way that I felt.

I knew that in my heart that I didn't exactly think that it was the right time for us to have a baby in the first place, still yet, I would have never wanted anything bad to happen to it.

But I had to admit that I was just a little relieved.

I wasn't sick anymore.

I was able to sleep longer than two hours at a time, and most importantly, finally, this chick was able to eat.

The baby had me so sick that I couldn't keep anything down, hence was why I'd lost almost forty pounds in only a matter of weeks.

Though I was thankful for the slimming
process…I was hungry!

But now I was eating again, and feeling a
whole lot better.

I could always get pregnant again; one day,
though it wouldn't be anytime soon.

Finally, after thinking over all of the details, I
turned onto my back and turned my head
toward Shelton.

His back was still toward me, so I touched it.

Without hesitation, he turned around to face
me.

With just enough light from the moon shining
in, I could see the tenseness of his face.

He looked so angry; so overwhelmed.

It was as if he blamed himself for what
happened, or as if he was upset that this was
one of those situations that even he couldn't fix
or change.

Quietly, we stared into each others eyes.

For more reasons than one, I didn't feel the same connection that we once shared.

It was as if I barely even knew him.

He was changing, constantly, right before my very eyes.

Either that or he had just done one hell of a good job at pretending, until now.

"I love you," I said, because honestly, I truly did.

"I love you too, with all of my heart, you know that right?" Shelton asked in a low tone.

Of course I knew that he loved me; but I also knew that there was something that he wasn't telling me.

And it had almost cost me my life…twice.

I just knew that somehow it was all connected; with Shelton being at the core of it.

I only wished I had the nerve to ask him, but since I didn't, I simply nodded.

"We are going to be okay, I promise you that," he reminded me.

But I wasn't so sure.

"Will you be preaching Dianna's funeral? Do you think that you can handle it mentally, or even emotionally?" I asked him, hoping that by bring up her and the situation, if I was lucky; maybe he would unknowingly answer a few of my unanswered questions.

I still didn't have a clue as to how they'd actually known each other.

For years, they both had lied to me; and though she was gone...I still wanted to know why.

"No. I found out today that she was cremated," Shelton said.

What?

She had only died three days ago, never had I known us black folks to have taken care of death so fast!

And to not even have her a funeral; really?

"How is that possible Shelton? Who had her cremated? So, you mean to tell me that they didn't have a proper service for her? How are her friends and family supposed to pay their respects? And who in the heck is *they*? " I asked him in disbelief.

"They had a private ceremony for her at St. Johns; even I wasn't informed of it until yesterday," Shelton whispered.

Damn it...that's it!

No more lies!

"Shelton, why are you lying to me? I'm supposed to be your wife!" I yelled at him, beyond frustrated.

Enough was enough!

"What are you talking about Maxi?" Shelton asked lifting up his head.

"Dianna was *not* Bishop Clarence's daughter. When I couldn't get a hold of her, I went to St. John's. I figured if anyone knew where she was, her father would. Imagine my surprise to find out that she wasn't his daughter. Better yet, he didn't even know who she was...or you," I concluded, taking a deep breath.

The look on Shelton's face was unexplainable; indescribable.

It was clear that I had hit some kind of nerve. Shelton breathed hard, fast, like a bull about to chase after the man in the big hat; the one always holding the red flag.

If I wasn't mistaken, I could have sworn that I'd seen traces of smoke coming from his ears and from the top of his head.

"You did what? What right did you have to go there and ask questions? You had no right to go there!" Shelton screamed unexpectedly; startling me.

"I have every right to know the truth!" I shouted back at him as he got up from the bed and headed toward the bedroom door.

"No, Maxine, you don't! Damn...not everything is meant for you to know; nor is everything meant for you to understand. You are my wife, a Pastor's wife; know your place and play your role. Mind your own business Maxine…and stay the hell out of mine!" Shelton yelled, slamming the door behind him.

Well, I'd always imagined the conversation going slightly different that.

Oh, and by the way...he *boarder line* cursed--- again.

More confused than ever and not knowing how else to respond, I started to cry.

Now, I was sure that he was hiding things from me.

They both had been all along, and from the looks of it, Shelton had no real plans on telling me the truth.

Was my marriage, my life, one big, fat lie?

Instead of chasing Shelton for more answers that I was sure that I wasn't going to get, I snuggled back under the covers and looked outside at the pouring rain.

I allowed my tears to fall effortlessly, mimicking the actions of the rain drops.

I didn't have all of the answers, but there was one thing that I knew for certain...

I had no idea who the man was that I was married to.

And I had a problem with that.

~***~

"Look, Maxine, about last night…I didn't mean it," Shelton said to me the next morning at breakfast.

He had managed to make eggs, bacon and toast.

The pancakes and grits were both epic failures.

I didn't respond to him.

I kissed our daughter and took a seat.

"Dianna and I had a past that you or anybody just wouldn't have understood, okay?' Shelton said taking a seat beside of me.

At first, I thought about being nice, civil; but to be honest, I just wasn't in the mood.

"You're supposed to be a Pastor, Shelton…but you're not. You're a liar!" I yelled at him.

For a minute or two too long, Shelton didn't respond.

Out of nowhere, Shelton slammed his fists into the kitchen table, shattering the glass.

"Watch your mouth in my house Maxine! You are my wife and you will do what I tell you to do! The problem is, you think you know...but you don't! You don't know nothing Maxine; nothing at all! And I am a Pastor! I will not let you or anyone else, say otherwise!" Shelton stood up, as blood dripped hastily from his right hand.

Mackenzie started to wail and I jumped to my feet to get her, but Shelton stepped in my way.

"I don't want to hurt you Maxi, please don't make me hurt you. Please believe me when I say that all I have ever kept from you was for your own good. I promise you that it's for the best," Shelton became somewhat emotional. For just a second, I felt something other than anger toward him; I felt sympathy.

"How bad can it be Shelton huh? I'm your wife," I pleaded with him.

Though I was still begging for the truth, I was becoming more and more terrified of it.

Shelton allowed the shedding of a few tears, but soon pulled himself together.

He allowed me to pass by him and comfort our daughter, but still, he said nothing.

After Shelton started to clean up the broken glass and the ruined breakfast, I knew that the conversation was over.

If I could only turn back the hands off time…I would have done a background check on him…before I married his ass!

Maybe then, when nothing came up for him, I could have asked questions that either he would've answered; or I simply wouldn't have married him.

I've heard many say that everything that glitters ain't gold; well, I'm officially going on record to say that every Pastor leading from behind a pulpit…doesn't necessarily need to be followed.

You just never know who you are putting your trust into these days.

Look at me; I couldn't even trust my
Pastor…or my husband.

~***~

"Shelton, have you seen my keys," I screamed
in the direction of the phone.

Speaker phone was a blessing from the Lord.

That was my very thought, as I finished
pulling my hair up into a bun.

"I have your keys with me," Shelton replied.

What?

"Shelton what do you mean you have them
with you? Why do you have my keys?" I asked
him in frustration.

I wasn't in the mood for Shelton's crap today.

I hadn't been out of the house in weeks, since
the miscarriage and Dianna's death, and with
Mackenzie off of my hands, I was dying to get
out of the house and get some fresh air.

"You don't need to go anywhere Maxi. I'll see
you when I get home," Shelton said and hung
up the phone.

Was he serious?

What was I…his hostage now?

I called him back several times, but he didn't answer.

What was his problem?

What did he think that I would do; just take off and leave?

Trust me, if I really wanted to go, I didn't need my keys to do it; or any money for that matter.

Again, Mama always taught me that when things were good, stable, whatever you do, put back for a rainy day.

And I had done just yet.

Obviously, Shelton knew that things were really bad between us if he assumed that I might try to leave him.

Don't get me wrong, I'd thought about it…more than once, but at the end of the day, I still loved my husband.

From the very beginning, he had been nothing but good to me.

Even now, he still hadn't done me any harm; except for not being completely honest with me.

He'd said that it was for my protection, or for my own good; but I say, its bullshit!

Please, excuse my *French.*

But the entire situation was frustrating!

Again, I thought about Mama and her sayings, which was something that I had been doing a lot lately.

I'd been doing it so much that in a way, it felt as though she was using all of her resources from Heaven to try and tell me something.

Her words had definitely been heavily on my mind lately.

She'd always say:

Lying is something that is so easy to do, but the outcome of a lie is never easy to undo.

I wondered now, if she had been speaking from experiences of her own.

With her words in my head, I revisited my lies.

I'd lied about my first marriage; but really, it was for the best.

Besides, he was dead; it wasn't like he could cause any problems in our marriage.

I'd lied about my drinking.

But he was a Pastor…what else was I supposed to do?

Tell him that I loved a nice stiff drink after a long day of work?

I don't think so!

I felt I was more than fair with cutting all the way down to a glass of wine here and there.

It wasn't like I was getting drunk.

I'd also lied about the number of men that I'd let *play in my sandbox*; but that was only because I didn't think that he would understand.

I didn't want him to see me as some *Jezebel* or a woman who misunderstood how valuable and precious her *ruby* actually was.

I'd always known its value; hence is why I'd always tried to use it as though it had secret powers or something.

But nevertheless, my lies were small, compared to whatever it was that Shelton was hiding.

And let's be clear, those lies had all came before our marriage; I hadn't told a single one after...other then little white ones.

But at this point, I was over it.

If he wanted to keep a few secrets, fine, I would simply get a few *more* secrets of my own.

After all, divorce just wasn't an option.

I wouldn't do that to Mackenzie, and let's be honest; I just wouldn't do that to myself.

Two husbands were more than my share; and if I had any say in the matter, there wouldn't be a third.

I could only pray that things eventually, returned back to normal.

Pray.

Now, that's something I hadn't done in a while.

At that very moment, I fell down on my knees and I began to pray for strength, patience and anything else I could think of that might help me get through these *trying* times.

My life had been spared twice in only a matter of months, so it was obvious that I had a purpose.

I was sure that my life still had meaning, and no longer could I waste a minute of it, not even a second of it, wondering about things that I probably couldn't even change.

At this point, it was simply time to let go of all the worrying, wondering, confusion, and prying and just...move...on.

I just wanted a little peace…and letting go was the only way that I was going to get it.

I spent a few minutes more telling God all about my troubles and then I decided that I didn't need keys to go where I wanted to go. I could walk.

..

Forty pounds down felt good, and there wasn't any point in putting the weight and pounds back on.

Hopefully I could keep them off, so I changed my outfit, and my shoes, grabbed my phone, put some money in my bra and headed out the front door.

I had to leave the door unlock, but in our neighborhood, and with our nosy neighbors, I was sure that the house would be just fine.

Walking, I didn't have a clue as to where I was going, but I was okay with that.

I was simply enjoying my view.

I was especially enjoying the breeze as it played *tag* with the loose strands of my hair.

When I was a little girl, I loved the outdoors.

I could stay outside for hours.

I didn't have to be playing; I could simply just be sitting, listening, to all of the different sounds of nature around me.

The sound of birds chirping was something that I had always loved the most.

The way the clouds moved into different images or the way the trees always rustled in the wind always seemed to relax me.

My love for those things never changed as I got older.

Outside was where I thought and reflected on my life the most.

Briefly, I started to think about the attack and near death experiences.

You would think that I would have been scared to walk down the street; but for some reason, I wasn't scared at all.

No one was going to make me fear taking a walk on such a beautiful day.

No one, not even Shelton was going to keep me stuck in the house as if I was on house arrest; especially when I wasn't the one committing the crimes.

Although I did wonder if the stroll was too much for my body, so soon after a miscarriage, it was too late.

I was a block away from home and passing
right by the church.

Of course, Shelton was there… as always.

There was only one other car in the parking lot
beside his; one that I didn't recognize.

It was a tan Mercedes Benz.

I figured with a car like that, it must have been
someone very important.

It could have even been another Pastor.

Church members *loved* their Pastor's.

I know ours sure did.

They didn't mind coming together and
blessing Shelton in anyway that they could.

There just wasn't a price tag or dollar amount
on their love.

I passed by the church and continued my
journey up the street.

A few ladies of the church lived along the way;
but I didn't bother to stop by for a visit.

I didn't want anyone ratting me out to Shelton
so I headed to the community park.

I sat on a bench all alone and smiled at the children who appeared to be having the time of their lives.

They ran and laughed as a feeling of peace and joy entered my body and remained there for the next few hours.

It wasn't until the growling of my empty stomach that I figured that it was about time to head back home.

Stopping at a store along the way for a snack, and something cold to drink, I walked slowly, thinking about my marriage.

I decided that I was going to try getting through to Shelton one more time; but in a different way.

I was going to tell him about my deceased ex-husband and about the hundred plus men that I intentionally excluded from our conversations about past sex and lovers.

Lord, I wasn't exactly sure about telling him about my love of wine just yet; but I was prepared to if that meant that by hanging all of my dirty laundry out to dry, in return, he would do the same.

If he did, he did; and if he didn't...

I was done worrying about it.

As he said, I'll spend the rest of my life playing my role as a Pastor's wife and he can keep all of his skeletons in his closet and all of his secrets to himself.

I loved him enough to simply leave the past in the past and let it go.

During my walk, I'd also decided that I wanted to go back to work.

It was time to do something just for me.

Something that I actually enjoyed.

I need something to keep my mind from wondering and off of all of the drama.

Coming up on the view of the church; the first thing I saw was Shelton.

After all, he was wearing a loud yellow t-shirt; the one that the kids had made for him for a previous Youth Sunday.

The second thing I saw was a woman.

They were standing by their cars, chatting.
About what, I'm not sure since I wasn't within
listening range.
Neither of them noticed me, and before they
could, I decided to hide on the side of a house
across the street; the one right beside the
church.
I waited for her to turn her head back toward
the church and when she did; my heart fell out
of my chest and into my stomach.
It was her; the woman that had on the red
dress…who was now wearing a red blouse and
a black skirt.
She must have thought that red was her color.
Looking at her…it was.
Though I couldn't hear a thing that they were
saying, it appeared as though they were
arguing.
Better yet, just from knowing my husband, I'm
sure that they were.

There were tons of hand movements, head shaking, and she even jumped in his face a few times.

My blood was starting to boil as I saw Shelton ram his finger into her forehead and then grab her by the mouth, squeezing her at the cheeks. That was so out of his character...well then again, maybe I was watching the real him in action.

Was Shelton having an affair?

Assuming Shelton had gotten the best of her; she hopped into her car and sped off.

Tan...her car was tan.

My mind wanted to remember something, but it couldn't.

If only I could remember the color of the car the day that Dianna was killed.

Had the car been tan?

I really couldn't remember.

Focusing back on Shelton, he leaned up against his car as he watched her drive away.

He dropped his head, so I assumed that he was praying.

His hands were now in his pockets, which was always a sign that he was nervous.

What is going on?

Finally, Shelton got into his car and drove away.

Safely and unseen, I came from beside the house and continued to walk toward home.

Something just wasn't right.

Shelton just couldn't be having an affair.

He loved me too much…right?

And he was a Pastor for Christ's sake!

He preached on adultery all the time, surely he couldn't be committing it…could he?

And all of a sudden, this woman pops up.

She pretends to be a visitor of the church; and now she's having private meetings and arguments with my husband?

Oh hell no!

My mind and my heart went back and forth as to whether or not I should smack Shelton on sight.

With his temper lately, especially the one I had just witnessed, I wasn't so sure that smacking him was such a good idea.

But nevertheless, I had a right to know what was going on.

My back pocket began to vibrate, and I knew exactly who it was.

Shelton.

He was probably home now, and saw that I wasn't there.

He called over and over again, but I didn't answer.

Walking up our driveway, I spotted Shelton sitting on the front porch, still holding the telephone.

When he caught sight of me, he stood.

I walked toward him, trying to figure out what I wanted to say but before I could say a word, he spoke first.

"Maxi, didn't I tell you not to leave this house? The door was wide open when I came...I thought maybe someone---I want you to hear me and hear me good. I can't protect you if you won't let me. And before your blood is on my hands, I swear, I'll divorce you first," Shelton said and walked away.

I stood there with my mouth hanging open as he slammed the door behind him.

Huh?

The door was open?

But I was sure that I shut it behind me.

I was positive.

And Divorce?

Who said anything about a divorce?

~**********~

~You are the key to all of the doors in life that you wish to go through. Instead of focusing on finding the key that fits; sometimes you just have to change the locks. Change can be a beautiful thing~

Anonymous

Chapter Seven

"I would like to ask my beautiful wife to come up and give us a song selection," Shelton said, looking in my direction.

It had been a whole month since he had made the comment about divorce and since I'd seen him privately chatting with the nameless woman.

I still felt someway about it all...but I had said nothing.

Basically, I was doing what he had ordered me to do...play my position.

Yes, I was still salty about it; but I wasn't causing any trouble.

It was what it was, and was going to be whatever it was going to be.

For the most part, I guess, Shelton and I were doing okay.

Not better...just okay.

Trying to be understanding, I concluded that it must be something really serious for him to even mention the word divorce.

Pastors took marriage very seriously...as all people should.

The promote the vows regularly, that a couple takes before God, so it must be something major, if he would even consider divorcing me...just to keep me safe.

So, more or less, it was simply best to forget about my insecurities, questions and concerns, and trust my husband and take him at his word.

Maybe I didn't need to know certain things or every little detail about his past.

Maybe.

The mysterious lady in red, since that day in the church parking lot with Shelton, had been out of sight...but definitely not out of mind. Every Sunday, I looked for her but she hadn't shown her face.

Hopefully, whatever the argument between the two of them was; it was enough to keep her away---for good.

If there was something, anything, between them going on and if he wanted to keep living and preaching; it had better been over.

Pulling down my dress, I stood up and headed to the microphones at the front of the church.

I'd always been a good singer; not a great one like Mama, but still yet I was decent.

It had been a while since Shelton had put me on the spot, and for the first time, I was nervous.

I smiled at the crowd as I searched my heart for a song.

For some reason, I thought about the song that Lady Pauline was singing; the very first time I had come to the church; the same day that I decided to change my life.

With her sweet voice replaying over and over in my head, and with my emotions suddenly all over the place, I closed my eyes, and opened my mouth.

Many times, I've been broken.

Often used and abused.

Many trials go unspoken.

Often leaving me sad and confused.

But Lord if you put your hands on me,

And grant me just a touch of your Peace.

I know that I can win this race,

With the help of your mercy and grace.

Lord fix me, I'm broken, and I need to move on.

Tears flowed steadily down my face, and I sang with all of my might; and with all of my heart and soul.

The entire time I was singing I was thinking about Shelton.

I know; my focus was supposed to be on God, but with every note I sang, I became more and more overwhelmed with thoughts of what was going on in my marriage.

It wasn't until I was finished singing that I actually opened my eyes, only to see that the entire church was on their feet and giving God some praise.

Shelton was now, standing right beside of me; and once I placed the microphone back on the stand, he reached out his arms in my direction.

I hugged him as he began to whisper a prayer of encouragement and love in my ear.

And at the end of his prayer; he asked for my forgiveness.

He said that he was sorry for everything he had done lately.

He asked me to forgive him for causing confusion and frustration in our marriage.

My eyes filled up with tears as I shook my head yes, and as his hug grew just a little bit tighter.

This was the man that I fell so deeply in love with.

This was the man so full of love and goodness that I married.

This was my husband.

My peace in the middle of a storm.

My light when I couldn't find my way.

Shelton had been so many things to me, and I just couldn't imagine my life without him.

I headed back to my seat, smiling and thanking the Man above simply because I knew that everything from that day forward was going to be okay.

If only that had truly been the case.

~***~

"Who is it?" I asked, opening the door before I'd gotten an answer.

There she was...in the flesh.

The woman in red.

The woman from the church and the same woman that I'd seen having a private conversation with my husband.

Immediately, I went into defense mode.

If she said one wrong thing; she could consider her ass...*whooped!*

And she had come to my house, and knocked on my front door...oh she was a bold one!

But she could best believe that I was the right
one to give her a good old Southern beat
down.

I hadn't smacked a hoe in years; and I
definitely didn't mind smacking the skin off
the face of a home-wrecker.

"Who are you? And what do you want with
my Husband?" I asked her, getting straight to
the point.

My arms were folded over my chest, and I was
sure that I had done a few neck rolls during the
process.

She looked at me; strangely and even had the
nerve to smile.

I opened my mouth to say something; but
before I could, she spoke.

"You said what do I want with your husband?
Technically, he's just your Pastor; he's actually
my husband," she said with a smirk.

She pulled out a piece of paper from her purse.

She was hesitant at first.

As if she was thinking about her next move.

As if she knew that whatever she did next;
there was no turning back.

Finally, she handed me the paper; excuse me...
the marriage license.

Levi Maurice Tate and Shelia Claire Brown-
Tate were the names listed.

I looked at her confused.

"Oh, that's right; you call him Shelton…that
isn't his real name by the way. It's Levi, " she
said confidently.

You have got to be kidding me?

This was some kind of joke…right?

"This doesn't make any sense," I mistakenly
said aloud.

"Nope, it doesn't. But he's *my* husband...and if
you don't mind...I would like to have him
back," she said, snatching the paper from my
hands.

She looked at me in an unusual way.

I could see the heartache in her eyes, although
she desperately tried to hide it.

And I was sure that she could also tell that my heart was breaking, right there, as I stood in front of her face.

Her face softened, for only a second.

It was as if she wanted to apologize or say something comforting or sympathetic…but she didn't.

She simply turned and walked away.

I stood in the doorway, still in a daze.

Had I really just heard what I thought I heard?

Had I really just seen what I thought I seen?

I watched her drive away in her Mercedes, and still yet I was unable to move.

Shelton was married to someone else?

Shelton's real name was Levi?

Hell no, back to my original thought… Shelton; *my* Shelton was married; to someone other than me?

Huh?

This had to be some kind of joke!

She was wrong; she had made some kind of mistake.

Finally, I shut the door, and stood, facing the back of it.

I didn't know whether to cry, scream, or start messing some stuff up…so I did nothing.

For all of thirty minutes, I stood still, doing and saying absolutely nothing.

Suddenly, I got an idea and ran to my computer.

So, here's the back story.

With being the daughter of a lawyer; investigation just becomes a part of your life.

I would watch Mama for hours, at her computer, searching, looking for information or clues.

Of course, I knew of many and plenty of ways and sites to find whatever I needed, whether it was personal or public; with enough accurate facts and start up information.

I could pretty much find out whatever I needed to know; which was why I was so disappointed when I couldn't find my Daddy.

The only thing I could think of was that Mama hadn't been honest about his real name.

That was the only explanation.

And since he was *allegedly* dead before my birth; he never signed my birth certificate, so I had nothing else to go on.

But as for Shelton and this woman...I had all that I needed.

I searched the name from the marriage license.

Levi Maurice Tate.

There were a few results but they were all located in other states and every one of them were at least ten plus years older than *Shelton*.

So instead, I headed to a more private background check site and searched the name again...the results were the same.

Next, I searched her.

Shelia Claire Brown-Tate.

I was able to find her; minus the last name Tate.

She was born in California; but check this out…she'd lived in the same exact city in Texas that I had…for about two years.

Interesting.

I immediately started to try to figure out if maybe I had pissed her off back in the day.

Maybe I stole her man; or at the very least had sex with him.

But there was no way that I could pin point which man that it might have been; even if I tried.

Now, it was showing that she was located in Washington D.C.; where she had been for years.

Then what the hell was she doing all the way in South Carolina?

I grabbed my credit card and paid for the most expensive and advanced search that they had on her.

This search came with everything from traffic tickets, to bankruptcy…and marriages.

I headed to the marriage license section; but there was nothing there.

Huh?

There was absolutely nothing there.

I continued to look through all her information.

Her name was exactly what had been on the marriage license that she'd shown me---minus the last name Tate.

Tate was nowhere on her file.

The search even included a picture of her driver's license, so I knew that I had the right person.

What the hell was she talking about?

I headed for my phone to call Shelton, but I stopped in my tracks.

What was I supposed to say?

From the looks of it, the marriage license had been a fake---so what was I calling to say?

I put the phone back down and headed back to the computer again.

There was nothing connecting her to Shelton or to a Levi Tate.

Just what was she trying to prove?

I searched Levi Tate again, and even tried to narrow the name down to California and even Texas…nothing.

So obviously, from the looks of it…she was lying.

Was this her plan in attempt to get me to leave Shelton…so she could have him?

It was obvious that she and Shelton knew each other, in some way; but *how* was the question. Shelton hadn't been to Washington, so I couldn't help but wonder why she was here. There was no South Carolina address on her profile, not even under the relatives that were listed for her.

I also searched and paid to see her relative's profiles too; just to see if something was there. Her father's last active address was in California; her mother's was in Washington.

The other people listed were all along the west coast; either that or marked as deceased.

There was nothing tying her to Shelton under their information either.

She lived in Washington, but she was constantly showing up here.

I knew for a fact that Shelton just didn't have the time for some crazy long distance love affair, but there just had to be something that I was missing.

But what?

For the third time, I tried searching the Levi Tate again; and I even searched Shelton Cartwright again…nothing there.

I went through the relatives again, and then everyone that was listed on their profiles too.

By the time I was done, I had paid for over fifty profile searches and background checks and still; nothing connected a Shelia Brown to a Levi Tate or to a Shelton Cartwright.

"What are you doing?" Shelton asked startling me.

I hadn't even heard the front door open. Quickly, I exited out of everything that I could and turned around to face him.

"Nothing…how was your day?" I asked, but Shelton didn't look convinced.

"What were you doing on the computer Maxi?" he asked, avoiding my enthusiasm and question.

Think quick…

"If you must know, I was looking for a job," I said.

Yes, that was a good lie.

Shelton smacked his lips and exhaled.

"Maxi, we discussed this already. We said you wouldn't go back to work until Mackenzie was at least five," he said shaking his head.

Sucka'…he believed me.

"Okay, okay, fine I won't go back to work, are you happy now?" I asked playing along.

"Very," he smiled and kissed my forehead.

If only he really knew what I was up to.

~***~

There wasn't a day that went by that I wasn't spending hours at the computer, so called investigating.

I had even tried calling the numbers listed for Shelia, but none of them were in service.

I don't know about anyone else, but when a random woman shows up at your front door, claiming to be married…to your husband…somebody owed somebody some damn answers!

But for right now, and thus far, I had found out tons about her and her family; but not one thing about her and Shelton.

Maybe she didn't expect me to do my research.

Maybe she'd thought that I would automatically believe her and jump the gun, leave Shelton, so that she could have him.

Maybe.

But if there was proof…any proof to what she'd said; she had better believed…I was going to find it.

But so far, there was no proof and her story just didn't add up.

Mentioning anything to Shelton was pointless. For starters, I didn't even know if she was telling anywhere near the truth and if I was wrong, Shelton and I would be right back in the same stage that we had just come from, and it would be all my fault...again.

"You ready to go?" Shelton asked, interrupting my thoughts.

Smiling at him, I nodded my head.

The summer was coming to an end, and we were beach bound.

I was ecstatic to be getting away from all of the investigating and craziness back home.

I just wanted to forget everything that had happened over the past six months, and I just wanted to enjoy myself.

But as God was my witness, if Shelia ever set foot in our church or South Carolina again, and I saw her; I was going to drag her from the church, all the way back to Washington...or wherever the hell she came from.

And that was my good word.

Shelton reached over the arm rest and held my hand.

I smiled as though I was taking a ride with my high school crush; only Shelton wasn't nearly as bad as he had been.

My high school days were just as bad as my college ones.

I lost my virginity at the young age of fifteen.

I'm not proud of it; but I couldn't change the past.

When Mama became a lawyer, though she made time for me regularly; sometimes she just didn't have time to give.

My *first* was a pretty average kid---named Jasper McDowell.

He wasn't exactly popular nor was he exactly what we considered a nerd.

He was just a regular kid, and that was what I liked about him the most.

No, he hadn't been the only one to ever show me interest; but he was the only one that ever took the time to *pretend* as though he didn't just want my body.

Although we all knew that he did.

Secretly, I had a crush on him for quite some time and when he finally took notice in me, I tried my best to keep his attention.

When the conversations about sex started to arise, I did what I thought I had to do to make sure that he stayed around.

But of course once he had the bragging rights of being *my first*, he was gone, and I quickly became non-existent.

At first, my feelings were crushed but after a while, I figured that was the way it worked.

You use people for your own personal reasons; and then you dispose of them as though they meant nothing at all.

Needless to say, I followed the train that was always moving, and it led to countless encounters with boys and men who I allowed to use me as though I was nothing more than a piece of ass.

But that was then; now, I had a man at my side that despite the recent mishaps, he was indeed Heaven sent.

I didn't have to beg for his love, it was already mine.

And nobody, no Shelia in Hell, was going to take that away from me.

Forgetting the thoughts of the past, I kissed Shelton's fingers and allowed my eyes to tell him the words that I couldn't say.

We were the Cartwright's…together…forever.

~**********~

~Sometimes you have to go through the worst. To get to the Best~

Anonymous

Chapter Eight

I was sad that we had to return back to South
Carolina.

The beach had done us both some justice.

Shelton was able to relax and forget about
church business for a while.

I was able to concentrate on loving my
husband.

And Mackenzie had the time of her life.

Now, it was back to reality, as we passed the
church and soon pulled up at home.

Leading the way, Mackenzie and I headed to
the front door, while Shelton began to unload
the car.

Before I had even fully reached the door, I
noticed that it was cracked open.

"Shelton!" I screamed in his direction and he
dropped the bags and headed our way.

He entered first and we followed behind him.

I gasped at how empty it was.

We had been robbed.

What wasn't stolen was destroyed.

The furniture was either missing...or ruined.

All of our electronics, televisions, computers,
jewelry, or anything of value...was gone.

They even had the nerve to take all of our
damn food!

Our wedding pictures were ripped in half.

Our daughter's baby pictures had been written
on with black markers.

There was no doubt in my mind that whoever
had done this was no stranger.

There was no doubt in my mind that Shelia
hadn't had something to do with this.

Shelton ordered Mackenzie and I to go sit in
the car until the police arrived.

While sitting there, I noticed that my car had
four flat tires and that the front window had
been shattered.

This means war!

Shelia Brown or whoever the hell she
was...was mine...and I meant that!

~***~

We were staying at the house that I'd
purchased when I first moved to South
Carolina.

We'd kept the property and usually kept it
rented out; but just our luck, the tenants had
moved out only a few months before.

It was fully furnished, and though it wasn't as
lavish as the one that Shelton and I had just
moved from; it would do.

Our neighbors hadn't heard or seen a thing in
regards to our break in; which I couldn't
believe.

With all of the damage that was done and
especially being that we had the nosiest
neighbors in all of South Carolina, I found it
hard to believe that no one had seen or heard a
thing.

The church owned the home, so what was
destroyed was covered under insurance.

The material loss wasn't the real issue.

The issue was that someone was trying to get the best of us; and boy were they giving it their best shot!

And I knew exactly who was behind it all; and I was willing to bet that Shelton knew too.

Shelton decided that it would be a good idea to sell the house.

He said that he wouldn't ever feel safe enough to leave Mackenzie and I there alone again.

The church agreed to purchase another home for us to live it, but we were in no rush.

Surprisingly, Shelton wasn't pressing the issue as much as I thought he would be.

In a way, it looked as though he had no real plans to purchase a new house for us at all; well, at least not anytime soon.

So, for now, we were settled and comfortable in my---well our, two bedroom home.

Shelton and I cuddled, watching a movie, as Mackenzie slept peacefully on the other end of the couch.

I listened to the sound of Shelton's heartbeat, to see if it matched mine.

Looking up at him, I waited for him to take his eyes off of the TV, and put them on me.

Once he noticed that I was watching him, he looked down at me, and kissed my forehead. His kisses still had the power to make me melt, but I wasn't quite ready to *turn up* the heat.

"Shelton, can I tell you something?" I asked him, though I was mentally at a tug of war on what I actually wanted to tell him in the first place.

Keeping it real, I wanted to mention Shelia. Not so much as to tell him what she about them being married or whatever; but to attempt to ask him who she was...and how he knew her.

Everything in his past, really wasn't my concern, but when a potential past person was causing problems in the present, hoping to be a part of the future; correct me if I'm wrong...but that was worth mentioning.

Our relationship had been better than ever, so I could only hope that he would be more willing to open up to me.

It was as if all of the issues were starting to make us stronger, closer.

I didn't believe Shelia about the marriage piece; but I did believe that there was something.

"Yes," Shelton responded, still looking into my eyes.

"I lied to you about something," I said, and immediately tried to take back my words as soon as I'd said them.

Damn it!

That was not what I meant to say!

Can I have a redo?

But Shelton was all ears, there was no turning back.

Oh, hell, why not?

"I lied about something when we first met. I guess I didn't think that we would ever really get married, but we did. Anyway, sex partner wise…it kind of wasn't just two; well including you," I said ashamed.

Suspiciously, instead of being angry…Shelton appeared somewhat relieved by my confession.

It was as if he was expecting me to say something else.

There were a few lies that I could have chosen to be honest about, but I felt that this one was the easiest.

Maybe my new found honesty would spark something inside of him and have him come clean on a few things that I was sure that I needed to know.

Wishful thinking.

"How many more?" he asked curiously.

Now that was a question that I wasn't exactly ready to answer.

I pondered the idea of lying about the number but oh well, it was in the past.

"Well, um, it was two…plus maybe a hundred," I whispered.

I couldn't believe my ears...

Shelton started to laugh.

"What's so funny?" I asked him, offended.

He didn't answer me.

He only laughed for a little while longer.

After a while, he finally quieted down and looked at me with a smirk on his face.

I was somewhat pouting as I waited on his response.

"Don't you think I know a lie when I hear one?" Shelton asked, though he really didn't need or want my answer.

I was quiet, still giving him the evil eye.

"Look, I don't care about that. All that matters is that I'm the last man that you will sleep with," he said in an assuring tone.

And the best husband award goes to...

"Maxi, I lied to you about something before we got married too," Shelton uttered.

Bingo!

That's what I was waiting for!

I sat up straight, giving him my full attention. Yes! Finally he was going to be honest will me. "Well...I don't know how to say this. I don't know where to start, so I'll just come right out and say it. The truth is....at first....I hated your cooking! Thank God the Mothers of the church gave you a few pointers. Your food used to taste like card board!" Shelton proclaimed and fell out laughing.

I playfully punched him a few times in the arm.

Screw him...I could always cook!

I looked at him as he continued to laugh in my face, and then he returned his attention to the TV.

I was hoping that he would have been honest about something a little more *serious*, but whatever secrets that Shelton had, were locked away.

And from the looks of it...the key to his heart full of secrets...was long gone.

~***~

"Hurry up, or we are going to be late," I screamed from the car.

Never and I do mean never, had there been a morning during our entire marriage, that I had beat Shelton getting dressed for church on Sunday.

He went back into the house to change his suit, again; for the third time.

I wasn't sure about this, or if there was some kind of rule in the Pastor's handbook, but Shelton never wore the same suit twice.

Ties and shoes, maybe; but suits, never.

I checked my watch once more and then observed my surroundings.

I'd always like this neighborhood.

Its beauty was one of the main reasons I'd chosen the house.

All of the houses and lawns were well groomed, and it looked like the perfect street to raise a family and grow old on.

During my observation, I noticed a black car in the distance.

It was only about four or five houses up from ours, but on the other side of the street.

They appeared to be looking in our direction, but when they noticed my head hanging out the window, looking at them, they turned their head.

Eventually, Shelton came rushing back out of the house.

"Babe, do you see that black car right there?" I nodded in that direction.

"Yes…what about it?" Shelton asked and started to back out of the driveway.

"I think they're watching us," I said.

Shelton stopped on brakes and looked at me.

He shook his head and proceeded to drive.

"Go that way," I ordered him.

"Why? The church is this way," he said and pointed in the other direction.

If looks could kill, I'd just stabbed him like five times, no lie.

Shelton got the hint, and slowly drove pass the black car.

The driver, a man, turned his head just as we were passing by.

"What? Was he one of your two…plus one hundred men from your past?" Shelton chuckled.

I rolled my eyes at him, refusing to answer his question.

Whether Shelton saw it as strange or not; I would definitely be keeping my eyes open.

Church went by swiftly and smoothly.

Five people gave their lives over to the Lord and I did my part by taking down their names and numbers so that as the weeks went by, Shelton could give them a call to see how they were holding up and staying on track.

Once we were outside, and as I talked to one of the visitors, I spotted a tan Mercedes…and Shelia, passing by the church.

"I was wondering when you were going to show back up," I mumble under my breath.

Apparently, I was louder than I thought I was.

"Who?" Shelton asked behind me.

"Huh, oh, no one," I said as I kept my eyes on the car until it was out of sight.

Shelton turned me around and looked at me.

I gave him a fake smile that he questioned with his eyes.

He released my arms and said nothing.

I turned back around to continue my conversation with the woman standing next to me, but I wasn't exactly listening to what she was saying.

I was going to have to do a little more investigating; there just had to be something that I could use to my advantage.

There just had to be a way to get to Shelia; up close and personal.

And this time I would be prepared.

I wouldn't be caught off guard...I would be ready.

It was time to show little *Ms.* Shelia just who she was messing with.

~***~

"Honey, I ran into a Shelia at the grocery store today, and she asked about you. I didn't recognize her, is she from another church?" I lied.

I had become so obsessed with trying to find out everything I could about this Shelia Brown. I had half a mind to hop on a plane and go to the Washington address that showed as most current for her, but since Shelton would never go for that, I had to play dirty.

"Who?" Shelton asked, stepping out of the bathroom and into the bedroom.

"She said her name was Sheila---Shelia Brown," I repeated, watching every move that he made.

He only appeared uncomfortable for a split second.

"Hmm, the name doesn't ring a bell. I don't think I know a Sheila Brown," he said and headed over to the bed.

Lie number one.

I knew for a fact that he knew her.

I just didn't know *how* he knew her.

"Well, she was pretty sure about who you were and she recognized both me and Mackenzie. Guess who she reminded me of?" I replied as we both got under the covers.

"Who?" Shelton asked timidly.

"Dianna. At first I thought I was seeing a ghost. She looked so much like her that they could have been twins. I mean, there were a few differences, but for the most part she favored her quite a bit," I said, still keeping my eyes on Shelton.

There were a few minutes of dead, chilling silence.

"I can't say that I remember a Shelia; especially not one that favors Dianna. Maybe she has me confused with another Pastor," Shelton finally responded.

Lie number two.

"Maybe," I responded and kissed him good night.

I was going to get to the bottom of it all, even if it kills me.

~**********~

~Be careful what you wish for...because sometimes, but not exactly in the way that you prefer...your wish just may come true~

Anonymous

Chapter Nine

What a nightmare...literally!

I woke up in a cold sweat and with my heart beating what felt like a hundred beats per minute.

I hadn't had a nightmare like that for years; since after Mama died.

Desperately, I tried to remember every single detail...but it was gone.

But I did remember the basics.

Sheila was trying to kill me---again...maybe.

This woman was starting to get the best of me. My every thought was about her and who she was, and what she wanted, and if she wanted Shelton.

Though still, he wasn't showing a single sign of worry or infidelity, I knew that something crazy was about to happen.

I could feel it.

Shelton was still peacefully asleep beside me,
so I tip-toed quietly out of the bedroom,
closing the door behind me.
After getting a glass of water, I headed to
check on Mackenzie.
She was sound asleep as well, in the same
exact position as the grown man sleeping in
the other room.
She was getting so big, so fast.
It seemed just like yesterday that we were
bobbing and weaving through traffic, trying to
get to the hospital, hoping that I didn't deliver
her in the back seat.
Dianna was there, holding my hand, telling me
that everything was going to be okay.
I'd waited all my life to be a mother and
though contractions were of the Devil; I
wouldn't trade those few hours for anything
else in the world.
For years I'd thought that I simply couldn't
have children.

As many penis's that had taken my vagina for a ride, not once, not even my ex-husband, had I ever been pregnant. I guess Shelton and I were just meant to be and meant to make someone as beautiful and as smart as Mackenzie; together.

Closing the door behind me, I headed to the living room to take a seat, but decided that a seat on the porch would be so much better. The cool night air was sure to relax me and calm my spirit.

I opened the front door with one hand and flicked the porch light on with the other.

My heart almost fell out of my chest as a person in all black, wearing a mask, stopped dead in their tracks at the bottom of the steps at the sight of me.

I started to scream Shelton's name and the rather large figure turned around and surprisingly, ran as fast as a speeding bullet. And guess what they ran to?

The same, damn black luxury car that I'd seen parked, watching our house a few Sunday's ago.

Shelton was now at my side, as I pointed to the car as it sped down the street and turned left.

"What happened?" Shelton held me in his arms, and started to pray before I could even answer his question.

"I couldn't sleep and came outside for some fresh air. Luckily I came out when I did; someone, in a mask, was headed up the steps," I said, still struggling to catch my breath.

Shelton was still praying but prayer isn't what I wanted.

I wanted answers!

"Shelton, please tell me what's going on. All of a sudden strange, dangerous, things keep happening to us. It has to be for a reason and I feel like you know why," I begged him as he now secured the front door.

He looked outside once more and then turned to face me.

His eyes told me that he was trying to figure out if he could trust me with his deepest, darkest secrets, but at this point in time, he simply didn't have a choice.

"Sit down," he said softly.

I did as I was told and he sat across from me. He was still for a few moments.

My guess was that he had to figure out how to say whatever it was that needed to be said.

"There are a lot of things, about me, that I've never told you...or anyone. I hadn't always been saved Maxi," he said.

Well duh, I didn't have to be a rocket scientist to know that.

"I used to be into a lot of bad things with a lot of bad people, and I'm more than positive that they want me dead," Shelton said.

Okay...what?

"What? Shelton what are you saying?" I asked, now even more frightened.

"I'm saying that I'm not who you think I am. At least not entirely," he looked at me once

more and then got up and walked toward the
window.

He looked out once, but never turned back to
face me.

"Sheila Brown, *is* my wife...well she was," he
confirmed.

So the bitch was telling the truth?

Well I'll be damned!

"So you were married...before me?" I asked in
a harsh tone, though technically, we were both
guilty of the same lie.

Shelton was hesitant.

"I'm married to both of you...technically,"
Shelton commented still refusing to turn
around.

What the hell did he mean he was married to
both of us?

Isn't that illegal or something?

And besides that, how could he lie about
something like this?

And all of this time!

Before I could stop myself, I picked up the glass that earlier was filled with water, and threw it, aiming for the back of Shelton's head. Lucky for him...I missed.

"So, she was right...you are Levi Tate?" I asked him, now standing to my feet.

Shelton spun around so fast that just watching him almost made me dizzy.

"What did you just say?" he asked walking toward me.

"Yes, *your* wife, number two, or should I say number one, popped up at our old house one day with a marriage license saying that you were her husband but I didn't believe her! Obviously I should have!" I shouted at him and turned around and headed down the hall.

"When? Why in the hell didn't you tell me Maxine? Shelton yelled.

"No, the question is, why in the hell didn't you tell me?" I said to him, swinging my fists in his direction.

Shelton moved out of the way just in time to avoid the blow headed for the right side of his face.

"What else did she say Maxi? What else did she say?" Shelton demanded to know.

My mind was racing and my heart was breaking.

How in the hell was he married to both of us? And he changed his name?

This was all just too much for me to handle.

I sat on the edge of the bed.

I felt like I was going to be sick.

Shelton sat beside me and touched my hand.

"Get your lying ass hands off of me!" I screamed.

Here I was thinking I was married to a Pastor... when all along I had been married to a damn Devil!

"Maxi, listen, let me explain. I married Shelia, right out of high school. I wasn't lying about being an orphan, or bouncing around from family to family. That's all true. Shelia was my high school sweetheart. She loved me when no one else did. She had always been there for me. I felt that it was only right to make her my wife; so I did. Though I had dated her for years, it wasn't until after I married her that I found out the truth about her family. I didn't know that she was the daughter of the biggest, most wanted, drug dealer in California, better yet, the whole West Coast. Her father took me in like I was his own son, and for the first time in a long time, I felt like I was a part of a family. Of course I didn't have enough money to take care of his daughter to his standards so, he put me *on*. He taught me his whole operation. I knew everything and everybody that he knew. I was the man, behind the man. I was his son," Shelton took a breath.

So, I was married to a damn drug dealer? Man, not again...

Lord take me now!

"I wasn't necessarily out there hustlin'; I was more like the hustlers' supervisor. I kept tabs

on them, handled the money, you know, sh---
stuff like that. In a way, I think Sheila's Pops
knew that I didn't have the heart to actually be
out there on the streets. Deep down, I knew
that I was better than that lifestyle, but what I
wanted didn't matter. It was all about what
was best for Shelia," he said.

Ugh, if he said her name one more damn time--
-I was going to throw up!

"Shelia's father wanted to expand his
operation, so he knew somebody, that knew
somebody else in Texas, and he sent me and
Shelia to be his eyes and his ears, and to get
things off the ground," Shelton continued with
his eyes to the floor.

Texas?

I couldn't believe my ears.

That explained why Shelia had a Texas address
on her background check.

And to think that Shelton lived in the same city
as I did, for a few years, and never had we
crossed paths.

Hell, I was surprised that I hadn't screwed him to be honest...as I said, in my younger years, I got around.

Speechless, I said nothing and waited for Shelton to finish his story.

"Everything was going fine and then sh---things started happening. Long story short, Shelia's father and his connect in Texas, were trying to set me up to take the fall for the entire dirty, drug operation. I respected that man. I looked up to him. But he couldn't be trusted. It was every man for themselves; so, I cooperated with the police. The bad part was that Shelia's loyalty to her father was unwavering. She would have never taken my side over his. So, I knew I would have to leave her behind. We'd planned it for weeks; the Feds and I. I'd told Shelia that I was traveling for a few days, to follow a lead on someone that was talking about making some real money. I knew Shelia would mention it to her father and I also knew that Shelia's father trusted my judgment; and if it was about making money, he wouldn't question me on it. But the truth was that the FBI was getting ready to make me disappear. I was going into witness protection. I had given up all the information that I could on men that they had been after for almost a decade and they were about to make their move on everyone involved, including Shelia's father. Snitching was looked down on in the streets; and with all the big dogs in the game that I had turned over if I didn't get missing, I was going to be dead before most of them was even booked in the county jail. Never had I been the type of man to run to the police; but they left me no choice. I would have never betrayed her father. I would have given my life for him; but he had only been a sit down away from hanging me out to dry. Hell, I just beat him to the punch," Shelton stopped talking abruptly. It was as if he was giving me room to ask questions, but I had no idea where to begin. He took it as a sign to keep talking.

"I loved Shelia so much and I didn't want to leave her behind. The cops knew that she would make a few moves here and there, but they agreed to let her have her freedom because I talked. They'd even tried to convince me to get her on board and take her with me. She didn't have to know every detail. She didn't have to know that it was me who ratted out the entire operation; maybe I could get her to come with me. I had only been gone for a few minutes and I turned around to head back to the house to talk Shelia into taking this so called *trip* with me. I was going to convince her that this would be a fresh start for us but on my way back I saw her driving; going in the other direction. I followed her that day to a hotel. I watched her go into the room, and then I saw him pull up…her father's connect…Ricky," Shelton said.

Ricky?

I know he wasn't talking about my dead ex-husband Ricky!

"The police and the FBI were calling me left and right. They couldn't make their move until I was safe in their custody. But I sat there waiting, watching the hotel room. Ricky was amongst the men that I had given up to the FBI. He was also a part of setting me up to take the fall, along with Shelia's father, but sleeping with my wife was a whole different ball game. I loved Shelia. Never had I been unfaithful to her and I never expected that she would do something as scandalous as sleep with a man that was in my face every single day. He had taken away the only thing that I had left. I didn't know whether to kick down the hotel door and shoot them both, or walk away, knowing that I'd dodge a bullet. But my manhood, my ego...was bruised. I called Ricky. I asked him to meet me at one of our spots. And when he did, I shot him. I killed him, and drove away as though I hadn't done a thing. By the time I made it to my safe location to meet the FBI, they'd already been by my house and told me that they had *taken Shelia;* but I knew that that was impossible. I was sure that she was still back at the hotel, waiting on a dead man to return. They said that they had tried to confirm if she was on board but when I didn't answer their calls; they played it safe and went by the house to get her, just in case. They brought *her* in and I saw that they had actually taken *Shelby*....Shelia's younger sister, who was on college break and visiting us for the summer. Because they looked so much alike, they'd thought that she was my wife, forced her to go with them, just before setting our house on fire. But they had taken the wrong woman. *Shelby* was who you knew as....Dianna," Shelton said looking at me for the first time.

Huh?

What?

Let me get this straight.

First, Shelton had just confessed to killing my ex-husband Ricky.

Though he had been a blessing in disguise at the time, he was still...a murderer!

Oh, and if that wasn't enough...Dianna…was really *Shelby*...who was also Shelia's, his other wife...sister.

So, Dianna really was like Shelton's sister...more or less, she actually was.

What!

Just what in the hell was going on here?

Shelton was dropping bomb after bomb and I was about to explode!

Shelton opened his mouth to speak, again, and I felt as though I was going to have a heart attack.

How much more was there?

How many more secrets did Shelton have?

"We tried to tell them that they had taken the wrong woman; but it was too late. They had already released the fake story to the press that a husband and wife had died in a terrible house fire. The news, media, the police, fire fighters were all on board with making sure that the FBI had all of their tracks covered; with making sure that the world thought that we were dead. That same hour, the Feds made over fifty arrests...including the girls' father. They couldn't leave a trail, so the FBI set out to find Shelia, and pitched her a bogus story about Shelby being stuck in the house, and that I must have forgotten something, returned home and tried to save her. But they explained that we both perished in the flames. They had even placed my car back at the scene and corpses inside the house and everything. Next they told Shelia that they had been investigating the both of us for a while, and that if I hadn't died, I would have been going to prison. To get her on board with disappearing, they told her that I had been a part of a drug deal gone bad, and that some very bad people were after us, and were looking for us, so for her safety she needed to head back to California and never return to Texas. They told her that it was best that no one but family knew the truth about who she really was and for her safety, they would simply continue to allow the press to think that it was her who had actually died in the fire...and not her sister. Fearing for her life, Shelia agreed and did as she was told. They put her on the next plane back to California. Just like that, we were all dead in the whole world's eyes and Shelby, or Dianna as you call her, and I were shipped off to South Carolina. They changed our names, gave us brand new identities. They told us that we could never go back or contact anyone from our past. No friends, no relatives; no one for our own safety. Shelby at first was resistant, but she didn't exactly like being in the shadows of Shelia all the time or always being treated like a child. So, when the Feds agreed to make her a grown woman with her own everything...she hastily agreed. They wiped away all history of us. Birth certificates, credit history, marriages, traffic tickets, everything you could think of. It was like we were never born. They gave me the credentials of a college graduate and a license in ministering and stuck us in a church, telling us that this is now who and what we were. I was now Pastor Shelton Cartwright and Shelby was now Dianna Forney. They gave us more than enough money to live and then they went about their merry little way. Dianna never really knew all of the details as to what I had done...and she never even asked," Shelton walked out of the bedroom, after he'd finished his last statement.

I was as quiet as a mouse, and as angry as a size two pair of jeans would be if I tried to put them on this size twenty-two ass.

More than anything I felt betrayed.

I was frustrated; I was confused.

It was so much to take in all at once, and at any moment, I felt like I was just going to fall over and die.

I had so many more questions, but none of them compared to the most important question of all.

What in the hell was I supposed to do now?

Shelton returned with two sodas and his Bible.

Was he serious?

After all he had just said, he comes in with a Bible?

After handing me the cold beverage, Shelton opens the Bible and begins to read it.

I sat quietly, merely watching him in disbelief.

"Shelton?" I managed to say to him, but he held up his finger.

After a few more minutes he looked at me.

"Let me finish before you say anything. Its been far too long," he said and took a sip of his drink.

I only managed to shake my head.

"No, Dianna and I never crossed the line of being anything more than what we were...in laws. Though we were all alone and all we had was each other, we both loved Shelia enough

not to go there; so we made up the whole
growing up at the same church story and pretty
much became as close as actual siblings,"
Shelton started back babbling.

I'd asked for the truth.

I'd wanted the truth...and boy had I gotten it.
And Shelton was still giving it to me.

Still yet, it was just so much to take in.

"Initially, I became a Pastor by force...but
something happened to me in the process.
Something changed inside of me. Of course
from playing the role, I eventually decided that
I wanted something more for myself and my
life. I wanted a new start. So, I went from
playing the role...to becoming the role. My
salvation became for real. I was saved and I
was ready to change my life and live the life
that I was always destined to live. I convinced
Dianna that Jesus was the way, and together
we made the transition, and encouraged each
other every step of the way. Yet, even with
God in my life, I was lacking something and I

needed something more. I remember the day you came into the church. I couldn't believe that it was you," Shelton proclaimed, reaching now for my hand.

This time I didn't pull away.

"What do you mean?" I asked him.

What did he mean he couldn't believe it was me?

"You were Ricky's wife," Shelton admitted.

Hold up...what a minute...did he say what I thought he'd just said?

"I'd only seen you a few times on pictures. Some that Ricky had shown; others that the FBI had shown from surveillance that they had on him. I couldn't help but wonder why or how you ended up coming to South Carolina. But there you were....in the flesh," Shelton said.

So, this fool knew the whole time that I had been married before?

And he never said anything?

The deceit I tell you!

"Shelton, wait a minute, wait a minute...so you really killed Ricky?" I asked him, still in disbelief.

"Yes," Shelton responded as though he didn't really care.

"And then you knew the whole time that I had been married before, and to him, and you never said a thing?" I asked.

"Yes. When you lied about it...I assumed that you were attempting to forget your past; just as I was trying to do the same," he said.

I couldn't believe my ears.

But so much was starting to make sense.

"So you pursued me on purpose; as a get back to Ricky?" I questioned Shelton.

"Yes...maybe...a little at first. But by our third date, I was madly in love with you and there was no denying it. My decision to love you and make you my wife had nothing to do with Ricky," Shelton explained.

The biggest part of me had wished that the last thirty minutes had never happened.

I just wanted to forget every single thing that Shelton had just confessed to me.

Curiosity had definitely killed this here cat; dead.

I didn't want to know not one more thing or detail about Shelton...or his past.

"Shelia says that after her father's trial that put him away for life, she and her mother, decided to leave California. They took all of his money and settled up in Washington D.C. There, she says that she started her own real estate business, and a few months ago, she had a client who wanted her to see about purchasing a home here, in South Carolina. Sheila explained that she'd visited a good many of cities here in South Carolina and then one day; she came here. Just so happens, she was passing by the church and saw Shelby--- Dianna and I crossing the street to the parking lot. This was months ago. That day, Shelia jumped out of her car hysterical. At first, she

cried and hugged Shelby and then she kissed
me---"

"Kissed you?" I screamed, now pulling my
hand from his grasp, again.

"Maxi, it happened so fast, I didn't see it
coming. She'd said that it took her years to get
over the deaths of her husband and her sister. I
believed her about Shelby, but she was having
an affair on me; so she couldn't have possibly
truly loved me, the way that she was claiming
to. But after the initial shock was over, she
accused us of faking our deaths, and running
away to be together. So, just like I'm doing
now with you, I had to explain to her what
happened...my clean version of what
happened. Conveniently, I left out a few
details, such as turning over her father, but
more or less, I told her that we didn't have a
choice and that no one could know that we
were still alive. I even told her the story of how
the FBI made a mistake in taking Shelby,
Dianna, instead of her. After a hell of a lot of

explaining, Shelia believed me; but the bad news was that she wanted me back. She'd said that she'd never stop loving or thinking about me. She'd never remarried; but she did have a child," Shelton paused.

Oh hell no!

'Shelton, please don't tell me, please don't say it," I whined.

"Yes Maxi...*he's* mine," Shelton said.

I felt like someone had just ripped my heart out of my chest and stomped on it.

He had another child...and with her?

"At first, I didn't believe her, and told her that I knew about her affair; but I agreed to a blood test, and unfortunately, the results weren't what I'd thought they would be. I was the father," Shelton tried to wipe the tears from my eyes but I swatted him away.

"I'm so sorry Maxi...but there's more," Shelton said as I rolled my eyes.

"She wanted to know where we stood, and if we could be a family again; but I had to break the news to her that I already had a family; you and Mackenzie," Shelton exhaled.

I guess this is where all the trouble starts...

"I told her that I was happily married and that's when she flipped out. She wanted me back. She wanted me to be a family with her and Noel; my son, but I refused. I told her that I would never leave you. I told her that I would never give up the life that I had. I was a different man now. I was a Pastor, I had a wife and a daughter, a church full of people who loved me, and there was nothing and no one that could make me walk away from it. Let's just say; Shelia got angry," Shelton concluded. And then he went on to tell me about the threats and the secret drama that he had been through for the past few months; which of course I knew nothing about. He told me that he had to inform the FBI that Shelia had found out that he was alive; and that they had started to reach out more often in hopes of making sure that the situation didn't get out of hand.

And that's where the John fellow came in. He was really an FBI agent and had been informing Shelton of suspicious activity on Shelia's part. He had been keeping a close watch on us for quite some time and he was even the man that had been the eye witness of my attack. The truth to the story was that he had actually lost sight of me in the crowd and by the time he'd gotten to the parking deck; I was already on the ground. He described Shelia, but he really hadn't seen her attack me at all. Though they were sure of it, he couldn't prove it so they couldn't arrest her. Now, they feared that she had leaked the information of Shelton being alive to her father. According to Shelton, John had reported that the last few months, Shelia had gone to see her father numerous of times. If indeed she had told him the truth...we were all in danger.

Her father would have known that Shelton had to have something to do with putting him in prison.

And we all know what happens to a snitch.
Shelton also explained meeting her a little
while ago, at the church, at the advice of the
FBI, just to see where her head was. He said
that she was still angry. She'd said that she was
going to make him love her again and that she
wanted him to be a part of her son's life; and
that she would do anything to make it happen.
Shelton said that day she was so angry, that
she confessed to attacking me at the mall and
to the car accident that accidentally killed her
sister. He said that he believed that it had
really had an effect on her mental state;
because after Dianna died, she had gotten
worse. That day he'd recorded their
conversation and confession, and the FBI used
it to threaten her. They told her if she told
anyone, even her father that Shelton was
alive...she would loose her son and go to
prison for a very long time. And if she kept
quiet...they would wipe her slate clean.
Isn't it funny how some things work?

She would walk with murder...if only she could keep her mouth shut.

But with the random mishaps, I was willing to bet that the FBI's threats were already too late. With all of the news, or better yet confessions, I was a total wreck.

What was I supposed to say?

What was I supposed to do?

Most of all...what had I gotten myself into?

My husband was supposed to be a Pastor.

I was a Pastor's wife.

That's who I was; that's who I had become.

But it was all a lie.

My husband wasn't a Pastor...well okay, after five years, maybe he was; but he wasn't just a Pastor.

He was a liar, ex-drug dealer, murderer, babies' daddy and an adulterer...well, kind of.

I was so overwhelmed that all I could do was cry.

Crying wouldn't change anything.

Crying wouldn't make me feel better.

But at least if I was crying...I wasn't
talking...because the Lord knows how many
curse words I wanted to say.

~**********~

~Everything happens for a reason. And normally,
most of the time… it's for the best~
Anonymous

Chapter Ten

It had been days since our little conversation and things were still very awkward.

The tension was so thick that you *couldn't* cut it with a knife...you needed more like an ax.

There was always an elephant in the room and I still hadn't said too much of anything.

Honestly, I was still trying to digest it all and take it all in.

I wasn't exactly sure what I was going to do or what I wanted to do.

But I knew that eventually, I would have to do and say something.

The part that troubled me the most was that I wasn't even sure if Shelton was really even considered to be *my* husband.

Shelia had been right on the money when she said that technically *her* husband.

Technically...he was.

But then again, legally he was now my husband; and had been *involuntarily* divorced from Shelia a long time ago.

There were no records or acknowledgments of their marriage...but did God still acknowledge it?

I was so confused.

At least *my* ex was dead; therefore, my past marriage was dead.

Oh, and to think that his blood was on Shelton's hands...

Better his than mines.

But it definitely tainted my image of Shelton.

Shelton was supposed to be perfect...or at least close to it.

But he wasn't; he was a killer.

Was that something that I could get over?

Of all people, Shelton had killed Ricky.

Even though I was thankful that he had, Lord forgive me, but I just didn't know how to feel about being married to a man that killed the man that I used to be married to.

It freaked me out to be honest!

The drug life...I could deal with and get over.

I'd always expected that he had dabbled in the streets, or at least something close to it.

And Shelton had a son?

The jury was still out on that one!

I really didn't know how or what to feel about that one.

I guessed it was more so being stuck dealing with Shelia versus dealing with an almost six year old boy.

Every child deserved to know their father.

I was a firm believer of that.

Now, with Shelton's past coming back to haunt him, I was unsure if I wanted to stick around for the ride.

His delusional, *used to be wife*, had already tried to kill me...twice, so forgive me if I wasn't in the mood to stick around to see what happened next.

But through it all...I still loved him.

For now anyways.

Shelton, since he had come clean, was constantly running around in protective mode. He'd said that he had a bad feeling and that something was telling him that it was time to go.

He'd called the FBI agent, John---John Malone, to see about moving *us* to a different state. Though Shelton seemed to trust him, I still had one question in regards to this agent.

If he had been the man in the black car, watching over us and the house, for our protection...that night; then why had he been approaching the house wearing all black and a mask?

Why didn't he identify himself?

Why did he run away when I saw him?

Something just didn't add up.

"Call him again," I ordered Shelton to call John, who had failed to call him back in days. Whether I decided to stay with Shelton or not, I deserved for me and my daughter to be safe.

And it was clear that it was time to leave South Carolina behind.

"He didn't pick up, I'll leave another message," Shelton responded.

"No hang up," I said.

I headed to the computer and pulled up some contact numbers for the FBI.

After being transferred a thousand times, I was finally able to speak to someone in the correct department.

"Hi, I'm looking for Agent John Malone," I asked politely.

"I'm sorry ma'am, we don't have an agent by that name," the gentleman responded.

What did I tell you...I knew his damn name wasn't John!

"Well in that case, I need to speak to your boss; better yet...I need to speak to your *boss's*--- boss," I looked at Shelton as I spoke.

Leave it to a woman to get real results.

Come to find out, the agent's real name wasn't John Malone; it was Steven Curry.

He had been newly assigned to Shelton's case, after taking Shelton's initial call.

The question now was why he had given Shelton a fake name all this time?

No one knew; but every one vowed to find out. Nevertheless, it was discussed and we were promised around the clock police patrol as they prepared to relocate us within the next few weeks.

No one had seen or heard from Shelia.

But someone had attempted to burn down the church, so we were sure that she was still around.

The FBI was watching her place to bring her into custody; but she had disappeared.

We were getting a few random phone calls from blocked numbers, with no one saying anything on the other end, but other than that, things weren't all that bad.

Soon, it was time for Shelton to inform the church of his departure and prepare to hand down his position.

"How are you feeling?" Shelton asked me.

By far one of the hardest questions I'd ever been asked in my life.

"Honestly Shelton, I don't know," I said to him.

I studied his face and his body language.

I wanted to tell him that I felt like I was married to a complete stranger, but I didn't want to hurt his feelings.

I wanted to tell him that I was angry with him and that because of him, I almost died, twice, and because of him I loss our child, but I didn't want him to feel any worse than he probably already did.

So, I allowed my silence to say what I couldn't.

"I'm sorry that I wasn't honest with you, but I couldn't be. I tried to be so many times, but I just couldn't. Even that night that you thought I sleep talking; I wasn't. I was awake. I was trying to force myself to say it then...but it just wouldn't come out. I couldn't force myself to say it. But I promise no more secrets. I am the man you fell in love with. I am that God fearing man that you are proud to call your husband. I promise that I'll spend the rest of my life making it up to you...if you let me," Shelton promised.

See, it was when he said things like this that made me want to forget the obvious and ride with him until the wheels fell off; but it just wasn't that simple.

Maybe for him it was; but it wasn't for me.

I managed to force myself to smile in his direction, but I knew that things would never be the same.

No matter how bad he wanted them to be.

Another thing weighing heavily on my mind, was the fact that he only approached me; pursued me out of revenge.

I know, he says that he fell in love with me; but had it not been for what Ricky had done...would he have even noticed me?

"You know, I remember telling Shelby--- Dianna, the day that we landed here, that I wasn't sure if I would ever get married again. I was just going to start my life over and live for God. Surely I didn't deserve a second chance at life...and especially not love. A killer, drug dealer like me, didn't deserve a second chance; but nevertheless, He had given me that and so much more. I made a promise to Him that I was going to take this Pastor thing seriously. And then there you were. I fell in love with you and all I wanted to do was make you happy. God and you were all I needed. I never felt anything near what I feel for you---for Sheila. You are my one true love; you were created just for me. You have to believe that," Shelton came closer to me and fell to his knees.

Damn it...I believed him.

I didn't want to; but I did.

"Pray with me," Shelton suggested.

Prayer was definitely worth a try, so I joined him on my knees, and silently, we bared our souls to the Man above.

~***~

It was our last Sunday at the church and emotions were at an all-time high.

Shelton was a mess and so was I.

These people had been like family to the both of us.

We loved them, and they loved us.

They loved our daughter and we simply didn't want to say goodbye.

But we both knew that we had to.

It was for the best.

It was for our safety.

As Shelton preached his last sermon, I wondered what was next for us.

I wondered if we would be happy; or if Shelton would preach again.

We were informed that we would all have to change our names; and all of us would be erased from every record, just like Shelton and Dianna had been; just as though we never existed.

Luckily, I had no one looking for me, so it didn't bother me so much but I guess it was going to take some getting used to.

Mackenzie was still young so hopefully adjusting to her new name wouldn't be too difficult.

We were moving to Florida; and of course we were to never return to South Carolina.

We were also told that we couldn't keep in touch with anyone, which was going to be a little hard for both of us---especially Shelton.

We had to start all the way over…again.

I was trying to stay as positive about the situation as possible.

I'd always wanted to go to Florida, and now I would be living there.

I guess as long as we were together, that was all that really mattered.

Yes, I decided to forgive him and stand by his side.

After all, with Dianna gone, he truly had no one else.

Shelton and I were going to be just fine.

Shelton prepared to do the altar call and everyone stood to their feet.

Suddenly, out of nowhere...

"He's a fake! This man is no Pastor! He's a liar! He has a son that he doesn't take care and if you keep following him...he's going to lead you straight to the pits of Hell! He's a lying, conniving snake and a adulterer! This man is *my* husband...not hers!" Sheila yelled, pointing in my direction.

How in the hell had she gotten pass the patrol?

It was clear that she was drunk and she was dragging along side of her a little boy who looked identical to Mackenzie...minus the head full of her.

Yep, he was Shelton's alright.

The church filled with chatter as Shelia continued to make her way to the altar.

Shelton was as still as a lake right before midnight.

It was as if he was afraid that if he moved, he just might choke the life out of her.

Either that or it was because he had never seen his son before---in the flesh that is.

Even with the paternity test, he was swiped at a local lab and the swabs were sent off.

I followed his gaze as it toggled from Shelia to the little boy, multiple times.

Shelia continued to yell and expose Shelton for everything that he *used* to be.

She spit out every single detail that she could about his past and even went into her pocket to pull out he marriage license; waving it in the air.

I wondered why it hadn't burned in the fire along with everything else.

Ours was framed; before the *robber* ruined it; but maybe she had kept hers tucked away in her purse for whatever odd reason.

But nevertheless, she was surely proud of that piece of paper.

I looked around at the church members faces.

Some were faces of disbelief.

Others were faces of betrayal and frustration.

All were looking on, at Shelton; waiting for his next move or at least a response.

I had to do something, and I had to do it fast.

I had an idea, but this wasn't the place for it.

It wasn't the time for it.

What would everyone say?

What would everyone think?

And then it hit me, after today, I would never see these people again…so to hell with what they thought!

Shelia was so busy talking, yelling and screaming that she didn't see me approaching her.

But Shelton and the entire church did.

His eyes became as big as golf balls.

And just as Shelia turned around…

I knocked her ass out!

What…that was my lick back!

I asked the Lord to forgive me, grabbed Mackenzie by the hand and reached out my other one for Shelton to grab it.

He took off his robe, stepped over Shelia and grabbed my hand.

He stood for only a moment and then he turned to look at the little boy, who was now crying at the sight of his mother laying face down on the floor.

Shelton reached for his hand.

He only looked at Shelton at first; and then he looked back down at his mother again.

Shelton called him by his name and smiled at him and told him that it was okay if he took his hand.

After another minute of coaching, finally, he did.

Shelia didn't move.

I had knocked her out cold.

Maybe there, on that altar, maybe she would find Jesus.

The church was in an uproar as we headed out of the church.

Neither of us bothered to look back as we headed out of the double doors…

Bang! Bang! Bang!

I was still holding on to Shelton's hand as he fell to the ground.

Bang! Bang!

And I was *still* holding on to Shelton's hand…as I fell down beside of him.

~**********~

~The sad part about winning is…that someone else

has to lose~

Anonymous

Chapter Eleven

"Mrs. Jackson?"

I just stared at the man, who was reaching me a fan.

Oh, damn...he was talking to me.

Remembering my new name was harder than I thought it would be.

Instead of Maxine Cartwright, I was now Nora Jackson.

And my husband was no longer Pastor Shelton Cartwright...he was now;

Pastor Shawn W. Jackson.

That Sunday, months ago, Shelton and I were both shot; by the former FBI agent Steven Curry.

Come to find out, he was Shelia and Dianna's brother…from another mother.

Their father had been with women all over the place and apparently he had a few kids that he forgot to mention; at least to their mother.

Steven had always known who his father was.

And Shelia, being his favorite, had also known the truth for quite sometime.

Just so happen, the day that Shelton called to speak to someone about Shelia discovering that he and Dianna were alive and Steven had been the one to answer the call.

After looking through Shelton's files, Steven found out that he had been the one to put away his father.

Steven contacted Shelia and together, informed their father of Shelton's whereabouts.

Their father, knowing that Shelton had been a part of putting him away, ordered a *hit* on Shelton...and his family.

He had a few people who owed him a few favors; and Shelton's death would be somewhat of a settlement.

But Steven and Shelia promised him that they could get the job done themselves.

Steven didn't want anything to come back with his involvement; and secretly Sheila wanted to see if she had a chance at trying things with Shelton again.

Obviously, she loved him more than Shelton thought she did.

But things hadn't ruled in either one of their favor.

Shelton didn't want to be back with Shelia; and after our little conversation that day with the head honcho in charge, the FBI had suspended Steven until they could get to the bottom of his lies.

So, now, both of them hated Shelton...and wanted him...and me...dead.

But they both had failed.

I guess now they all could share stories; jail cell to jail cell.

After all, they all had a whole lifetime to bond...literally.

As for Shelton and I; we both lived.

Shelton was shot twice in his right arm and once in his shoulder.

Only one of two bullets fired in my direction hit me in my arm as well.

For an FBI agent, you would think that Steven would have had better aim.

We'd heard that he had never missed.

Not even once.

He always got his target.

But I guess we had a *man* named Jesus on our side.

Either that; or Steven felt some kind of internal connection, and wasn't as comfortable killing his *sister*...as he'd thought he would've been.

That's right.

I was Shelia's; Shelby's (Dianna) and Steven's...long lost...*sister*.

I'd known for quite some time now.

I'd discovered it a while ago, during the time that I had been doing all that research, background checking and investigating on Shelia.

One day, while looking at their father's record, Paul Ray Brown, I came across an address that was familiar.

It was the address of the house that I had grown up in, back in Texas.

It also showed that the same year that I was born, only a month or two before, a California address started to pop up on his record.

I discovered a marriage license for him; and he wasn't married to Mama.

It was obvious that they had an affair.

Whether Mama knew or not initially; I'm not sure, but at some point, I'm assuming that she found out.

That had to be the reason why Mama *killed* him off and that also had to be the reason why he never tried to find me or at least be a part of my life.

Or maybe he did; and Mama just wouldn't let him.

Mama had even lied about his name.

The few times she had mentioned it, she had called him *Ray Paul Lowery*.

She had simply flipped his first and middle name---and given him her last name.

So, after I put two and two together, it wasn't hard to figure it all out.

I knew that it was him.

I had found my Daddy.

When everything hit the fan, I thought about telling Shelton...I really did...I really wanted to; but really, what was the point?

We couldn't change much of anything, and there was no real way to undo or fix the situation.

The most important thing was that now, after searching for him my whole life, I knew who my Daddy was...and now I could spend the rest of my life---*forgetting* him.

Shelia was arrested and sent to prison for attempted murder, hit and run, and for the murder of *our* baby sister.

In a way, I guess that could have been the reason why Dianna and I had always had such a special connection.

But never would I have thought that we were actually *connected*.

As for Shelia, sometimes, in a way, I could almost relate to her and if I wasn't careful I might even find myself feeling sympathy for her.

I could see how she would have wanted her *husband* back; a *husband* that she felt rightfully belonged to her; a husband that was forcefully taken from her.

But I simply couldn't justify her actions.

Not hers... or *our* father's; or *our* brother's.

So, they were all people of the past and apart of the memories that we had left behind us in South Carolina.

Now, the four of us; Shelton, Mackenzie, Shelia's son and myself, were all adjusting to the Florida beach life; and I for one, had not one, single complaint.

Shelton had found another open position for a Pastor and he was now the head Pastor of Hidden Valley Baptist Church.

The church applauded as he stepped up to the podium.

He glanced in my direction and smiled.

I couldn't have been more proud of him.

His past was behind him and I could see the light of Heaven shining down on him.

This is what he was born to do.

This was why God had spared him.

This was his testimony.

I looked at him with more love and respect than I ever had before.

There he goes...

My Pastor...*and* My Husband.

~*********~

~Romans 3:23 King James Version (KJV)
[23] *For all have sinned, and come short of the glory of God~*

Jesus

~***The End***~

Note from the Author

Passion has always been my passion and I appreciate the opportunity to share my writing with you.

I absolutely love to write and I love my readers.

Thank you all for coming on this journey with me.

Email me: bmhardinbooks@gmail.com

or at info@savvilypublished.com

Twitter me: @BMHardin

Facebook me:

www.facebook.com/authorbmhardin

Check out my other books:

Dirty Bonds

Every Woman has a Price

Can You Stay for Breakfast?

The Wrong Shade of Lipstick

Mrs. Jones.